acclaim for kevin canty's

h o n e y m o o n

"Tight, exquisitely plotted stories. . . . [Canty's] prose has a terseness that belies his gift for lyricism."

"Beautiful and exceptionally well-written. Canty is an accomplished master of the short story form."

"Using crisp dialogue and mordant snippets of internal monologue, Canty brings his characters to life with revelatory magic."

kevin canty

honeymoon

Kevin Canty is the award-winning author of the short story collection *A Stranger in This World* and the novels *Into the Great Wide Open* and *Nine Below Zero*. His work has been published in *The New Yorker*, *Esquire*, *GQ*, *Details*, *Story*, *The New York Times Magazine*, and *Glimmer Train*. He lives in Missoula, Montana.

also by kevin canty

A Stranger in This World
Into the Great Wide Open
Nine Below Zero

kevin canty

honeymoon

and other stories

Vintage Contemporaries

Vintage Books

A Division of Random House, Inc.

New York

FIRST VINTAGE CONTEMPORARIES EDITION, DECEMBER 2002

Some of the stories in this book have appeared, in different form, in the following
publications: "Honeymoon" in *The New Yorker*, "Little Debbie" and "Flipper" in
Glimmer Train, "Red Dress" in *Tin House*, and "Sleepers Holding Hands" in *GQ*.

The Library of Congress has cataloged the Nan A. Talese edition as follows:
Canty, Kevin.
Honeymoon and other stories / Kevin Canty.—1st ed.
p. cm.
Contents: Tokyo, my love—Aquarium—Flipper—Honeymoon—
Carolina beach—Red dress—Sleepers holding hands—Little Debbie—
Scarecrow—Little palaces—Girlfriend hit by bus.
1. Love stories—American. I. Title: Honeymoon and other stories. II. Title.
PS3553.A56 H66 2001
813'.54—dc21 00-047979

Vintage ISBN: 0-375-70800-6

Book design by Terry J. Karydes

www.vintagebooks.com

Printed in the United States of America
10 9 8 7 6 5 4 3 2 1

For Lucy

Contents

honeymoon

and other stories

Tokyo, My Love

Some scenery, then: a sleeping city by the ocean, streetlights and foghorns, a wisp of fog curling down the hills (in fact cigar smoke, blown by a production assistant just off camera). Unbeknownst *to the citizens, a group of lit windows in one of the tall towers, busy with buzzers and maps, people shouting in Japanese: the command post. The tiny princesses are kidnapped. The missiles are racing into place.*

I am the thing that happens next.

I feel myself evolving. You of all cities, Tokyo—you must know what this feels like, the little fishing village somewhere near your heart, the layers of houses and shopping and industry accreting, century by century, to form your black pearl. . . . You are not what you were. You are not what you will be.

The rockets are gathering in the suburbs, and I am changing.

To go from one body to the next, to watch your wings develop out of nowhere, beautiful, spotted wings, to feel the many segments of your abdomen contract and swell, swallowing the hundred tiny legs—too many of them!—and then one morning the new strong legs under you, holding you up. I am beautiful. Your tanks can't stop me.

I know: Two men with mustaches have the princesses locked in a cage somewhere in the city, two near-Americans in business suits, etcetera. The princesses will be fine in the end. They will sing to me again, and I will go back to my island.

But all that is later. All that is plot. This is the moment that I love, this right now: the city sleeping, waiting, my body evolving, everything about to happen and the calm before. I can feel the city, there in the dark, waiting. I can feel how much you want me, Tokyo. Without me, without the thing that is about to happen, there's no escape from the chain of days, turning clothes into laundry and then washing the laundry, folding the clothes, stacking them away. Who could stand it? Who could love a life like that? Admit it: You know what I'm talking about. The thing inside you that wants a hurricane, a fire a flood, that wants to hear the beat of giant spotted wings, my wings, bearing down on the city, the jets of flame spewing from my mouth and the helpless tiny planes as I bat them to the ground. You want to see the tanks roll into the street, the long sentence of Japanese that translates somehow into the single word: "Fire!" Admit it: That's what you're doing here, isn't it? some tiny homeopathic dose of the hurricane you want, so that you don't choke on your own boredom. You want tanks and burning buildings, rail-cars flying, rocketry and gasoline, the prehistoric scream—out of my lungs, Tokyo—that will burst every ear that hears it.

Not yet.

This is my moment, the moment before. These are my beautiful wings, unfurling. You wait, unsleeping. You wait for me. I am the thing that happens next—to you, Tokyo. Tokyo my love. To you.

Aquarium

The crab is dancing slowly, delicately, across the bottom of the tank on several of its long unlikely legs. Eight feet across is Olive's guess, if there was room for the big king crab to spread out, which there is not. This seems cruel to Olive, though better than crab cakes, crab salad, Crab Louie. The legs wave like some remembered nightmare, shiver and purse together. They meet at a knot of shell and lump, some part of which must be a face. Olive looks for eyes, then looks away.

"Those things live in the Sound, here?" she asks her nephew.

"I don't know," Robbie says in his sleepy, lumpen voice, deliberately stupid.

This is what bothers Olive: the way the whole world has turned into a David Letterman world, where it's OK to be stupid. "You've never been here before?" she asks.

"A couple of times," Robbie says.

"But you've never bothered to read the signs?"

Robbie looks up at her, sleepy and grinning. "I guess I didn't," he says. "I just came to look at the fish, before."

"A resident of the coastal waters of Alaska and the North Pacific," she reads. "Can grow up to twelve feet in circumference. I'd hate to meet one of these babies in a dark alley."

Robbie looks at her like she has suddenly lapsed into pig Latin, this antique gangster slang. Olive sometimes feels a hundred. They move along, under the shadow of the great blue whale.

What makes it worse, Olive thinks, is that she has become the exact person that David Letterman makes his jokes about. She is originally from Indianapolis, for one thing, though she lives in Houston now. She is single, well-educated. She has no reliable sense of humor and she is in organized recovery. Lately she follows the straight and narrow path, though she does know others; in the family she's famous for cocaine. A souvenir of her one try at marriage, but the reputation sticks. When her sister heard that Robbie was taking heroin, for example, Olive was called on to jump on a plane and head for Seattle, a living example of the dangers. Maybe she could communicate with him in a way that the others could not.

"This is my favorite part," Robbie says, leading her into a dark-lit tunnel, his skin luminescent in the ultraviolet. Here, in the black tanks, are the things that live at the bottom of the ocean: blind fish, misshapen squid, starfish, tiny crabs, bodies formed and deformed by permanent dark and permanent cold. Olive is shivering again at the thought of it. They should have left them down there!

"Why?" she asks him. "Why do you like these ones?"

"I don't know," Robbie says. He grins at her and blinks, reflexive, automatic. All this boyish charm is starting to annoy her.

"It's like they're not even from Earth," Robbie says, "not even another planet or something but like another *kind* of planet. You know?"

"I *don't* know," Olive says. "Try it in English."

"I don't know," Robbie says, his face deflating in the black light.

Olive is immediately heartsore, because she did, in fact, see some glimmer of an idea there, because she had just put him down for no reason. But it was so easy! That was the problem.

"Why are we fighting?" she asks him. "I just got here."

"I'm not fighting," Robbie says. "You're the one in a bad mood."

"Maybe I should get an espresso or something."

And Robbie grins at her and there he is, right there,

Robbie. He looks at her as if it really never mattered. Happy puppy, Olive thinks. Playtime for pup.

Except: these are his favorites, these unsightly unspeakable tentacled things from the bottom of the ocean. Not the otters, not the slippery seals. These things dredged up from the residue of bad dreams.

"I want to look at the mammals," she says to Robbie. "I wish to see something with skin."

"Fish have skin," says Robbie.

"With fur, then," Olive says, still feeling the willies along her spine—those eyes, those pale fins. "I want to see something with hands and a face."

"We should have gone to the monkey house, then," Robbie says, following her out into the light again, into the air outside, pearly with rain, and across the concrete walkway to the otters and seals. They walk down a concrete ramp, under the water itself, and a hundred thousand tiny salmon swim between them and the sky. The fish shift and scatter like music, like silver electrons.

"This is what I like," Olive says, settling in front of the seal tank, the underwater part. And right on cue, a big seal swims by, inches from her face, twist-turning at the corner of the pool and then shooting past Olive again. He looks for all the world like he's lying down and leaning on his elbow as he glides by. He looks like he's smiling at her. He looks like he's showing off. "Don't you wish you could swim like that?" she says. "It's like flying, isn't it? It looks like flying."

"I went scuba diving once," Robbie says.

Olive waits for the rest of this statement, but apparently that's all there is.

"All that equipment," Olive says, "I should think it would be rather clunky."

"Oh, no," Robbie says, "no big deal, not once you're in the water. It's that whole thing, where you're like, usually you just think in back and forth, you know? and side to side. This way you get the up and down, too. It's a trip."

"I'm sure," Olive says, restraining herself. She's learning to translate.

Robbie moves his hands like Superman, flying, his body following. He says, "It's a whole new way to move."

They watch the seals, from underwater and then from above, watch until the other tourists drop away and the screaming children and teenagers on dates (magnetism of bodies, straining toward each other through all that Gore-Tex) and then, for a minute, it's just Olive and the animal bodies, she can almost project herself inside, sleek and fat and fast as a stooping hawk, bearing down on the unsuspecting salmon, the speckled sea trout, the unsuspected glide and then the sharp teeth cutting into the silvery skin. . . .

. . . and then the place reasserts itself, decaying fish heads on the floor of the pool, tourists (but Olive is a tourist herself!) in golf outfits, the sound of cash registers from the gift shop.

"I'm going to go back to the hotel for a minute," Olive says. "Take a little rest. I'm tired from the trip."

"I'll walk over there with you," Robbie says.

"Sure," says Olive, "thanks."

And then they're out on the waterfront, out in the cute city with the cute trolley cars and the cute ferries, a few small boats (do they hire them?) dotting the Sound with white sails, the gulls wheeling as the tourists feed them french fries by hand.

"Oh," says Olive, "I'm getting so cynical in my old age."

"These are the ones I like," Robbie says, nodding toward a pair of junior-high punks—flannel shirts, fresh piercings—walking unhappily down the waterfront, a careful ten feet behind their parents. Robbie says, "Here I am in Seattle! Where's Kurt Cobain?"

"Oh, be nice," says Olive.

"Hey, wait a minute," Robbie says, "isn't Kurt Cobain dead?"

"You could be from Milwaukee yourself," Olive says. "In fact, you *are* from Milwaukee, I believe."

"And proud of it," he lied.

They move in and out of the schools of tourists (a faint plant-sprayer mist in their faces and a pearly gray sky above), backing up at traffic lights and then shooting forward with the green, up the long hill climb and into the city walkers downtown, faster, full of purpose. The hotel is only a few blocks. Everyone is very nice in the hotel. Yellow walls, and fresh flowers in every room. Robbie follows Olive up in the elevator and then waits expectantly while she fumbles for the plastic key—red light green light, and then the faint tumble of lock cylinders. . . .

. . . and then she's up against the wall, his body pressed against hers, his tongue in her mouth, in the dim twilight of the room, the gray, underwater light. His hand under her dress. His tight chest through the cotton of his shirt.

"I thought we were going to be good," Olive whispers.

"This is good," Robbie says into her neck. "You want me to stop? I'll stop if you want me to."

"No no no," she says. "Not at all. It's wonderful to see you."

Robbie grins at her, leads her toward the bed, unpeeling as they go.

"Remember," Olive says. "Easy. Nice and easy."

~   ~   ~

Olive is not particularly fond of operations but she has had two optional ones. At twenty-four—against the advice of everybody in the universe—she had her tubes tied, tired of birth control and certain that she would remain child-free, a decision which she has not yet (thirty-eight this year) regretted. Two years later she went in for breast reduction. This is the one she still feels twinges over, too much vanity, too much looking in the mirror. But on balance that operation was a success, too. She had always felt too big and floppy, and now she looked more the way she saw herself: compact, trim, an easy mover. This was the way she was always meant to look.

Which makes it possible, in the afternoon light, to lie un-embarrassed with a boy who lifts weights, to drink red wine from a bathroom glass and admire his fresh tattoo, a cir-cling band of Celtic thorns around his upper arm, spiky and sharply cut.

"It's beautiful," she says. "It suits you."

"Thanks."

"It's going to look like hell in twenty years, though," Olive says. "I don't know why I say these things."

"Because you're supposed to," Robbie says. "You're here to help me, remember? Get me on the right track."

Olive feels a deep fright hearing him say this, a sudden sharp lurch of her organs. This is wrong, wrong, wrong, and they are bound to get caught. What started out as nearly forgivable (a wedding, too much to drink, a little fooling around, and then the invitation from Olive up to her hotel room, she still feels a little thrill at the memory of it, that long awful moment after she had asked him and then the rushing relief of his "yes") has now become intentional, criminal. Olive is the grown-up here. She knows, she can practically recite from therapy: It's OK to have this feeling, anybody can have a feeling like this, this rushing, tidal. . . . But it's not OK, it's never OK to act on that feeling.

The secret of adult life, Olive thinks. The secret to OKness.

But everybody else gets to act on their feelings, she thinks (furtively, wrongly, the injured child), and how come I can't? Olive is the only one playing by the rules, and where does it get her? Alone, in a house, in Houston, which (as somebody said when she moved there) is like living inside a cow's mouth. Why can't she give herself this little sweetness? After all, biology doesn't care: no two-headed babies, no babies at all. If Robbie doesn't mind. . . . Again, the little voice reminds her: It's OK to have the feeling, it's not OK to act on it.

But what if she doesn't care about being OK? The unspoken premise of all that therapy, that a sane reasonable normal life is what Olive wants. Really this is what she wants, this right here: the line of dark hair running south from his navel, the way the small of his back curves toward her and away. What's she supposed to do with this feeling? Where could she put it so that it wouldn't rot and fester and turn her sour?

I want what I want, she says to herself. I don't care where it comes from.

"I love men's bodies," Olive says. "Yours in particular."

"I'm glad," Robbie says.

"Sometimes I think I'm strung out on them," Olive says. "I keep it under control. Sometimes I think it's too bad that men come in them."

"Don't say that."

"Present company excepted," Olive says. "Although every one of them seems fine at the time, while it's happening. It's only afterward."

"I love women's bodies," Robbie says, "and I like women, too. I like the package, and I like the present inside."

"That's because women are better than men."

"It's true," he says.

"It isn't true," she says. "That's all on the surface. Women are nicer than men because they have to be, that's all. They don't have any money, usually, or any power. The only way that women can get their way is by being attractive and nice. People want to get their way in the world. You knew that?"

Robbie laughs.

"What's wrong with that?" he asks her. "What other way would people be?"

"I don't know."

"I mean, what else is there?" he says, and grins, and moves his warm hand up the inside of her thigh, the smooth pale skin.

But it's too late; the blue is welling up inside her, the cold and loneliness, just thinking about the little packages of desire wandering all around her. The moment—coming out of college, a couple of years before she sterilized herself—when she saw adult life plainly, not through the eyes of a child, and saw a sea of random electrons, silvery tiny fish moving in response to things they didn't understand, poor impulse control and worse impulses. People say it—"blue"—like it's supposed to stand for something else, but for Olive it's just a literal fact, a blue that fills her chest, that makes her heavy and slow and stupid. Stupid girl. . . . She reaches for him, she kisses his nipples and his neck, holding on like a drowning woman until she feels his body unfold, turn toward hers, respond.

~   ~   ~

Later they try to agree on dinner.

"I'm on a trip," says Olive. "I want a little something nice, you know, out of the ordinary. A nice dinner and some company. What's wrong?"

"Nothing."

"You don't sound like nothing."

"I'm just a mutt, you know," he says. "I go into those places and people look at me. Plus, I don't know."

"What?"

It's nearly dark now, his face unreadable. She could turn the lights on anytime, turn the nice hotel room back into its square, reassuring shape.

"I want to be your secret," Robbie says in the dark. "I don't want to be your boy."

"What does that mean?"

"Oh, you know," Robbie says. "Out in the fancy restaurant and everybody's looking at me, they think, you know, you're taking care of me. They see you picking up the check."

But I'm your aunt, Olive thinks. I have an absolute right to take you out to dinner and pick up the check. But the word "aunt" scares her, and she doesn't say it; too sharp a shape on what's between them. She realizes—a little guilty start—that she's counting on Robbie staying hazy, his usual mild fog. Olive thinks he will flee once he figures out what's going on.

Robbie, yawning. "I'm hungry," he says, pulling his pants up over his slim hips, no underwear, she notices.

"Wherever you want to go," Olive says, "whatever you want to do."

"Well, that's pathetic," Robbie says.

"That's me, pathetic," Olive says. "Let me take a quick shower first."

"No, come on."

"Why can't I take a shower?"

"Nothing," Robbie says. "I just want to go. I like you this way," he says, sitting on the edge of the bed, turning the light on and then reaching down to caress the base of her neck, the short stubble of her hair. He says, "I like you a little messed up."

Sudden terror of the light. She panics, seeing his body—his shirtless, beautiful, decorated body, tattooed and pierced (only in the earlobes, though) and exercised and firm, and she can feel her every scar and dimple, every dry striation. No longer nude but naked, under his eyes.

"I don't like to be gross," she says.

"Yes, you do," Robbie says, touching her hip. "A little."

"I'm going to take a shower anyway," she says. "A quick one."

"Can I smoke in here, then?" he asks.

"I don't like it when you smoke."

"That isn't what I asked."

"Open a window, then. If you have to."

"I don't have to," Robbie says. "I want to."

"Why are we arguing today?" she says. "All day, it's been like this."

"We're not arguing," Robbie says.

~   ~   ~

Then they're in a Chinese restaurant the size of an airline terminal, a dim room, red as the inside of a womb, and nobody is over thirty, everybody is smoking and nobody is ugly except the ones who make themselves ugly on purpose. A sullen slouch is automatic, draped over the red vinyl banquettes. Occasional fake movie stars in peroxide and leopardskin, thirties suits and bowling shirts—enveloped, Olive thinks, in a fog of sarcasm. Quotation marks around everything. I don't belong here, I don't belong here.

"It's funny," Olive says, "I always start out thinking I'm right."

Robbie doesn't say anything, lighting another Marlboro.

She says, "I always start out thinking I'm right, but it's always you in the end."

"What does that mean?"

"I don't know," she says, and sips her whiskey sour. Robbie ordered for both of them, and this is what she ended up with. She shudders to think what food might be coming for them.

"You just do what you feel like, don't you?"

"Only when I can," he says, and laughs.

"I always think that's wrong," Olive says, Miss Earnest, Little Miss Schoolteacher. "I always think that I'm the grown-up, you know, that I've learned all the right lessons. And then I see you, and I see that I'm the one who's screwed up. I've forgotten how to want things. I don't even want what I want. It's like I'm leading somebody else's life."

Robbie gives her his usual lazy grin, then swoops his hand back over his head, making a swishing sound with his breath. *Right over my head,* he's telling her.

"Be back in a second," he mumbles, and wanders off toward the back of the restaurant, where the bar is, where people—boys and girls of Robbie's age—are standing together and talking and blowing smoke in each other's faces. I don't miss it, Olive thinks, feeling warm and well-oiled and recently fucked. I don't want to *be* a twenty-year-old again, she thinks. I just want to sleep with twenty-year-olds. She settles into the red vinyl banquette, the bowling-alley tuck-and-roll. The plastic sticks to the back of her bare thighs in the sweet-and-sour heat. Olive is relaxed.

But then it has been ten minutes, and Robbie isn't back, and then twelve. She peers into the dim bar, seeing the faces of strangers. They rise up through the sweat and smoke like mercury. Alone, her agent gone, her ambassador, she doesn't belong. The waiter comes and sets two plates in the center of the table, one candy apple–red and the other gravy-brown, and the smell of the food nauseates her, and still he doesn't come. She cranes her neck; she twists and turns like a cuckoo clock, every couple of minutes, looking for Robbie. Not just old but pathetic, she tells herself. I am ridiculous.

And then she sees him, and she can tell—even from this distance, across the room—that he is fucked up. Robbie has been in the bathroom. Robbie has met somebody.

"Ah," he says, sliding liquidly into the booth, "food."

"In a manner of speaking," Olive says.

He hears the sharpness in her voice and looks up at her, busted. "What's the matter?" Robbie asks.

Olive shakes her head.

"What's the matter?" he asks again, grinning.

And now, she sees: she can't call him on it without disappearing, exiled again into adult-world, land of Mom and Pop. Where they don't, she remembers, want her either.

"I want some," Olive says.

"What are you talking about?"

17

"You know what I'm talking about," she says, "some of what you've got."

Robbie looks at her, his cool dissolving like sugar in water, a watery, panicky look in his eyes.

"I don't know what you're talking about," he says. "I just went to the can back there."

"And I am Marie of Roumania," says Olive.

A standoff, then—a high-wire silence, everything balanced between them. Olive is as scared as he is but better at hiding it. Robbie, on the other hand—Robbie really doesn't care. People who think they're going to live long and happy lives don't get tattoos like that.

"OK," he finally says. "I spent all my money, though."

"I've got money."

Robbie looks at her again—sideways, around the bend in his rubber neck—and she sees triumphantly that she is not Aunt Olive anymore or any other kind of known quantity. She has succeeded in scaring him. She is cooler than he is.

"Are you going to eat that?" she asks him, nodding her head toward the awful food.

He snaps out of his dream for a moment.

"That?" he says.

"You ordered it."

"Yeah," he says, "I guess I did."

"Let's go, then," Olive says. "We can eat someplace later, if we feel like it."

Robbie ponders, drooping. Finally he says, "My friend, he left."

It takes Olive a moment to interpret.

"Oh," she says, "your *friend*. Where did he go? Or she, I suppose."

"This other place," he says. "A club, you know."

No, I don't know, Olive thinks; but this times she remembers not to say it, not to squander her hard-earned capital of cool on the cheap pleasure of being right. Robbie wobbles out of his end of the booth. Olive leaves a twenty, hoping it's enough, and then remembers not to care. I remember how to play, she thinks. Just don't look down and you won't crash. She's wearing a tight, short skirt and a little top, and, if she doesn't look like Jayne Mansfield or Courtney Love, at least she doesn't look like somebody's hippy mother. She's small, compact. She can do this, she tells herself.

"Fucking shit," Robbie says on the stairs outside.

"What's the matter?"

He looks at Olive as though he doesn't recognize her, as though he's never seen her before. Then his eyes clear, and he laughs.

"Fucking spins," he says. Rain collects in his hair, tiny droplets that reflect the streetlight. "I thought I was going to fall down the fucking stairs."

"Maybe you should eat something," Olive says.

And Robbie grins at her: More advice, you lose. Thanks, Aunt Olive.

"Where's the club?" she asks, annoyed at herself.

"We can walk it," Robbie says. "It's maybe five, six blocks, no big deal."

The street: Olive remembers the blank stare of the passing cars, the eyes of the world on her, sixteen. Wild nights! The feeling that she was being tested, things were waiting for her, everybody would be watching, to see if she was truly cool or another of the disposable many. Several dozen different kinds of trouble. And here she is again. Olive feels a sudden sharp disappointment with herself, a blue shiver: the same street, the same blank passing cars, the same rain, the same dangerous boy at her side.

"In here," says Robbie.

"Where?" asks Olive. There isn't a sign, a light, a marker of any kind, just a rusting steel industrial door in the side of a brick warehouse, a muted, amniotic thumping coming through the walls, felt rather than heard. A faint trickle of fear. Now she has to do what she said she was going to.

"It's still too early," Robbie says, shoving open the door and letting out a furious chain-saw racket. He says something else as Olive follows him inside, but his words are lost in the din, the red lights, and cigarette smoke. She pays for both of them, and a cartoon demon stamps their hands with ultraviolet light, then says, "Hey" to Robbie, and they nod at each other. Boy or girl?

Onstage, some horrible teenagers are torturing an amplifier to death. It's dark and it smells. The crowd—not even a crowd but a scatter—stands motionless on the dance floor while the band hops and skitters. *Zombies*, Olive thinks, dressed in black and black, pale skin and tribal tattoos, little rebels all alike. Olive feels quite the dowager, and at the same time strangely younger, lighter. Why don't they dance? Why don't they lighten up?

"Fucking opening act," Robbie shouts into her ear. "You want anything to drink?"

Olive shrugs. Anything will do.

Robbie waits—for what, she cannot tell. Then she remembers that he doesn't have any money. She reaches into her small purse—is it the only purse in the room?—and finds her wallet, and wonders how much this will cost her. Robbie takes two twenties from her hand and waits. She hands him a third, and he goes, somewhere, leaving her alone at the edge of the dance floor. A little mild shoving and bumping is taking place, up by the band, and the rest stand in their trance.

Olive is either nine or ninety. Either way she doesn't fit.

The band stops playing, without a word, and starts to pack up their equipment. The stragglers on the dance floor disperse back to their tables, or to wherever they go, lighting cigarettes and not talking. In the smoky quiet, Olive can hear the scrape of chair legs against the concrete floor—then, as if the silence was to be feared, more guitars erupt from the speakers on either side of the stage, speakers the size of refrigerators, the music starting midsong, without introduction, so loud it makes her jump. What is wrong with me? she thinks. What has gone so wrong in my life that I have ended up here?

Without the pretty lights, the room is just more black-on-black, drab and sour. Robbie is nowhere. Olive is alone. She can't decide whether to stand or sit. She can't decide whether to stay or to go. Everybody else is outside. Everybody's left but her and the roadies, or whatever they are called—sweaty boys in black T-shirts, moving amplifiers around, saying, "Check, check" into microphones.

"You want something?" a little punk girl asks her.

It takes Olive a moment to realize that the girl is a waitress. What do I want? she thinks. What don't I want?

"A gin and tonic, please," she tells the girl, who looks at her, unbelieving, like Olive has just ordered a glass of blood or Drano. She moves off anyway, toward the back, the bar presumably, wherever Robbie disappeared to. I might as well sit down, Olive thinks—and then, for no good reason, says it out loud: "I might as well sit down."

"What?"

She jumps. It's Robbie, back from wherever, with two bottles of beer between his fingers. Now he's in control. Now Robbie's cool.

"You sure you want to sit here?" he asks, handing her one of the bottles.

Olive puts it on the table. "I ordered my own," she says. "You were gone so long."

"Ah," says Robbie, smirking at her. Oh, thinks Olive, oh, oh, oh. I have made so many mistakes.

"I found Larry," Robbie says.

It takes Olive a moment to figure out what he means by this: I found Larry. One if by land and two if by sea. The eagle flies on Friday. Then remembers.

"Where?" she asks him.

"He's in the bar."

"No, where do I, um . . ."

"Bathroom, I guess. That's where everybody else does, anyway." He slips the tiny folded packet into her hand, under the table. "Be cool," he says, "this is some shit."

"Like half of it?"

"Not even that," he says. "Wake up dead. Start off light."

Then Olive is sitting in the stall, the moldering rock-club bathroom where many have vomited, and she has the little packet open in her lap and she is staring at the white powder inside like it will tell her something.

"Come on," a girl says outside. "Hurry up, would you?"

And Olive, in a kind of mild panic, watching herself, wondering what she's doing and why, rolls the dollar bill into a tube and picks a tiny spot of powder off the corner of the paper and sniffs it delicately up her nose.

"Oh, Jesus Christ," says the girl outside, "junkies and toilets, the eternal romance."

Olive, eyes tearing from the chemical-solvent burn in her central head region, refolds the tiny paper and flushes, as if the world didn't know. This girl outside is Chinese, tiny, dark and bitter. She rushes past Olive with spit in her mouth, ready to fly.

How do I feel? Olive wonders. She dabs a spot of powder off the inside of her nostril, her face dark and strange in the filthy mirror. I feel pretty good, she thinks. So far, anyway. Her hips feel oiled, unsteady but smooth, as she meanders toward the tiny table at the edge of the dance floor where Robbie is bobbing his head, watching with blank eyes. A rising flood of warm water. A nice chair and a nice drink. Robbie looks up at her and he can tell, he smirks, but it's not mean. He's no better than her and she's no better than him.

Something is happening, though.

The barrage of noise coming out of the speakers stops abruptly, the lights come up on the empty stage, sparkle of cymbals in the multicolored lights, and psychically all the smokers know it's time to come back into the club, and there are more of them, drawn like moths to the light of the stage. And then some other music starts, unidentifiable, with violins and little faraway drums.

"This is Newman's idea," Robbie says. "I heard about this."

A woman comes out from the side of the stage, a woman even older than Olive in a red ruffled dress with flounces and heavy, cartoon makeup and a large silver triangle on which perch a half-dozen birds. Each bird is a different color, blue, orange, purple, like a pack of Lifesavers. She sets the triangle on a stand at the center of the stage and takes the red bird off its perch, holds it out toward the crowd and it takes off, flying in slow circles above the heads of the audience. A couple in the crowd start away in fear, another reaches to grab the bird, but the red bird twists away and keeps flying the same slow circle, joined by the blue dove, the green dove, the white dove. Soon all the birds are circling overhead, a rolling, dizzy motion.

"I don't feel that great," says Olive.

"It's OK," Robbie says; and she thinks, sure it's OK with *you*. But she stops her wobble by leaving the birds alone and watching instead the face of the bird-woman, the mask, the deep-red lips and the powder-white brow and the eyes set deep in black lashes. Her eyes circle the room, following the birds, but apart from her eyes, her face doesn't move, not a trace of feeling or intelligence or life; a mask, Olive thinks, behind which, some-place, a woman is living.

You and me, she thinks.

Then the bird-woman purses her lips, and, one by one, the birds fly up and land on her—her shoulders, her outstretched arms, finally, the last one, the red one, perches on her head, and the music stops. There's a woman with a bird on her head, Olive thinks, but something about her posture, her absolute dignity and stillness, keeps Olive or anybody else from laughing at the bird-woman. Slowly, an outbreak of applause takes over the crowd. But the bird-woman seems completely indifferent to this, too. She whistles again, and the birds fly onto their metal perch, and she walks off in profile, enveloped in her dignity.

The band comes on behind her. The band begins to play. The band is unbelievably loud, so loud it resonates down inside the center of Olive's body. She rises, along with Robbie. They move toward the music, as they must. They merge into the crowd, into the envelope of sound, the wall of guitar noise that surrounds them. *I'm living in the jungle,* shouts the main boy. He's huge, cloudy eyes, in a black raincoat. A couple of pretty boys for helpers. Olive feels the beat in her backbone, in the small bones of her throat. She feels her heartbeat shift, conforming to the drums. Robbie there beside her and both of them inside. No need to move or to explain. Olive—suddenly—*understands.* She's where she needs to be.

Flipper

Something's gone wrong with the boy. It's easy to see: his face (once lovely, elfin) is cased in a block of suet now. Wings of fat droop over his belt, shiver when he moves. Eleven years old. Little fireplug, roly-poly, Mama's little fatty. When he bends to find his shoes, the rolls of flesh on his stomach meet in dolphin lips.

His mother said it and his sister overheard. Now it's just his name: Flipper.

Summer evenings, freeze tag, fireflies, War, lemonade and sleep before dark. At bedtime, the name of Flipper is called from child to child, through the alleys (creosote and new wood, the smell of fences, everything new and naked), the woods at the end of the road, all the way to the comics-and-candy store on Hudson Avenue where he is trying to make himself disappear. Baby Huey.

Then they are driving all the way to Pennsylvania, his mother, his father, and Flipper. His sisters have been left behind. No one should be forced to see the camp for fat children, none but the punished. A hundred Flippers! Spare the girls! He sits in the backseat, alone, watching the telephone wires gallop from pole to pole, trying to hypnotize himself. Grim necks of his parents. This is New Jersey, 1964, the cars of the Kennedy assassination. He doesn't dare speak. Flipper is hungry.

At camp, there is no common misery but a hundred separate ones, no two alike: Baby Huey, Little Lotta, Porky, Tubby, Flipper. They tip the canoes on impact. They stare at their dismal breakfast bowls: oatmeal, plain. They have swimming practice, like giant cabbages tumbled into the water, their noses fill and bleed with green lake. Harmonicas, campfires. In the absence of their everyday tormentors, they quickly organize themselves into bullies and victims, and fight over smuggled Milk Duds. Two boys are caught "fucking" and sent home. There are bed wetters. Flipper has the top bunk. When the counselor shuts the lights off, the room fills with quiet sobs, they sleep on damp pillows. Once in a while, the telltale rustle of wax paper. All ears alert.

One day Flipper goes for a walk in the forest. The counselors call it "hiking." Alone: The fat campers are solitary, each encased in each. Ridiculous in shorts, and knowing it—his legs are pink as pigskin despite weeks of sun—he clambers over logs, hops from rock to rock to cross the creek. He dreams that this path will lead him to a Rexall store, a place of comic books and candy, an hour of comfort. His soft and secret heart. He lies on the bank of the creek in the morning sun and feels the warm grass springing upright again, tickling his neck. Almost time to go back. He pictures his lunch: an orange dome of canned cling peach on top of white cottage cheese, like a mockery of a fried egg. Fried eggs! And dry toast, when all he dreams of is butter, butter and Heath bars and marshmallow Easter chicks. Bitter and small and hard. The idea takes shape in his brain, then, a wisp of smoke and then the hazy outline and then the idea: He is not going back.

Dead by the road. Anywhere. You'll be sorry.

He doesn't run, he *couldn't* run. The stumps and switchy branches reach to trip him, the smell of skunk cabbage fills the marshy bottoms like a gigantic fart racing after him. Poor Flipper! They will picture this escape when he's dead. They will see they were wrong. The emptiness inside him, the place where lunch ought to be and snacks, and the love of his mother, and softness, this empty place contracts and loosens around a burning core. Damaged organ. Unlovely wobbling. After half an hour he heaves himself over the last fence of the camp and into the forbidden world.

His skin is covered with a fine damp sheen of sweat and his thighs are starting to chafe, a little. Dying will be even worse.

He fights back tears, girl-tears. The lumps of flesh on his chest, his father called them man-tits. A girl, an ugly girl, a fat girl. Flipper does not need a tormentor. He does not need help.

In an opening in the forest, not far from the lake, he comes across a girl who is also weeping. The terror of being looked at stops his own tears, the distant, longed-for call to heroism.

Are you lost? he asks, stepping out of the trees. She shakes her head, still nestled in her arms and her knees, won't give him anything. Her voice comes muffled through her dress: Go away!

I don't know where I am, he says.

Well, go away anyway!

He stands rooted in the meadow. She weeps again, head shaking, burrowing into her dress. It's checkered red-and-white, like a tablecloth. Screaming, splashing from the lake: other children having fun, the ones from the Baptist camp, the Boy Scout camp, the rich camp. Her hair is blond and cut abruptly at the neck, and on her neck are two small red spots, remains of pimples, so she's older. Is something wrong? he asks her.

This time she looks up, and her face is swollen and round and covered with pimples new and old, and she is enormously pregnant. How could she draw her knees up around that belly? The dress concealed her. Two years older than Flipper, maybe thirteen. Her belly rests between her legs like an enormous stone she has swallowed. I hurt my baby! she wails. I didn't mean to!

What?

Can't answer; not now. Buries her face in her dress again

and weeps, head shaking, clasping her hands so tight that her fingernails make white half-moons in her palms. Can you do that? Flipper wonders. Can you make yourself bleed? Thirteen and pregnant. He's never thought about this. Opens her face to him again and says, You won't tell anyone?

No.

Opens her dress and a lapful of candy spills out, all choco-late, little Halloween bars of everything: Hersheys, Nestles, Peter Paul Mounds. He can't stop staring, though her lap is nothing he should be seeing—the primitive bulge under the silvery-brown candy. She says, They told me not to but I couldn't help it. I'm so bad. They told me not to for my baby!

The silence, wind in the trees and the splashing screaming happy children, voices torn into the wind like scattered paper. You're all right, he says. You didn't do anything bad.

Miranda!

The voice comes distantly through the forest, then closer, the adult voice, counselors, footprints breaking on the brittle leaves. Take these! she says, all frightened, pushing the candy into his hands, scooping the little silvery bits into his greedy hands. Flipper is rich! Ten or twenty little candies, they over-stuff his pockets, he looks down and sees the tops of her breasts through the loose neck of her dress—blue-veined and milky white. Now go! she says, and Flipper goes.

Watches from the edge of the little clearing. A nun and then another nun come out, say something he can't hear. The full-dress model nun, with the hats and so on. Flipper squats, terrorized, Jesus will point him out, radio under the starched headdress, radar, they know—they have to know. Still he can't help following when they leave with her. A nun, the pregnant girl, another nun, like prisoners in a war movie. Pockets crammed with candy, he steals through the woods, following the white flash of the nuns and the red of her dress, a safe distance behind. Looking for what? He won't tell himself. Pizza face, preggy, the bulgy blue-veined skin. Not far from disgust, not far from himself. Pasty-white, fatty, Baby Huey. White frame houses through the trees; he thrashes closer, breaking twigs. Nobody notices him.

Through the scrap and scrub at the edge of the forest, he sees green lawns, green shutters, porches, a swimming pool. Chaise longues on the lawn, a pregnant girl in a swimming suit in each, six or eight but he's not counting. Some kind of treatment? They aren't happy, they aren't talking. These are the two-piece kind of bathing suits, so their bellies shine like moons in the light. Flipper wants to cry. On the porches, on the lawns are pregnant girls, in bathing suits or tent dresses—one of those modeled after a sailor suit, navy blue with white piping . . . and the nuns like moving telephone booths, walking on invisible legs, keeping track. Guarding against pleasure or happiness.

They lead Miranda into one of the buildings and then, a few minutes later, lead her out again, this time wearing a bathing suit herself. They lead her to a longue and she lies, on her back, with her eyes closed but not sleeping. Not wanting to see. The blue veins stand out clearly on her breasts, the parts he can see, and on her thighs. Humiliation. He watches from the edge of the forest until he gets a feeling: She knows he is there, knows he is watching. Then turns, and starts back for the fat camp.

~   ~   ~

What kind of boy is Flipper? He hides his treasure in a hollow tree, a hundred yards from camp, though squirrels might find it. The little bars are soft from carrying them in the pocket of his shorts, almost melted from the damp heat of Flipper. He allows himself one, a Hershey, soft as velvet on his tongue. Leaves the lump of chocolate in his mouth, lets it melt to nothing. Bliss. He closes his eyes, feels the sunlight on his skin. A face in the darkness. Hair as soft and blond as a baby's, No More Tears. She was fucking, really fucking, there is no other explanation; the thought makes him tremble. She had outgrown the small sins of children. Someday soon, he thinks. No More Tears. Holding the chocolate in his mouth, not swallowing, until the last taste melts away, eyes closed, concentrating. Then licks the wrapper clean.

Tells the counselors that he fell asleep in the woods. Either they believe him or they don't care.

The counselors were never fat. The counselors have beautiful, tanned bodies; they watch each other, the children disappear. Lesser species. Burning ants with a magnifying glass.

Canned cling-peach halves for dessert, cold from the refrigerator, they taste like refrigerator.

~   ~   ~

I'm not supposed to, Miranda says. They say it makes my baby excited.

It can't hurt anything, Flipper says. It's just a little bit.

I don't want to do anything to hurt my baby.

You don't have to, Flipper says, if you don't want to.

This time it's Special Dark. Slowly he unwraps the paper, then the foil, and slips the little sharp-edged square into his mouth, still cool and hard from a night in the forest. This time he carried it in a bag so it wouldn't melt. Ten-thirty in the morning, hazy blue sky, the sun warming toward the dust and emptiness of the afternoon. He closes his eyes but she doesn't go away; and in a minute he hears the rustle of the bag, the snap of a paper wrapper opening. He brought three for himself and three for her. No hurry. They have all morning. The edges soften, bittersweet.

There! she says. You can feel him, there! She guides his hand to the lower curve of her belly, presses her own hand over his. Through the soft cotton of her dress, he can feel her taut skin, bulging, ready to burst. She smells of soap and milk and medicine. Suddenly he feels it, the soft bone turning deep inside her, the baby. Instinct tries to pull his hand away, but she presses down, holds it close, and this time he feels a stronger shove, an elbow or a knee, something alive in there! A person inside you, Flipper thinks. A person inside me. His hand on her belly, inches away from her breasts, inches away from where she pees from, where the baby will come spilling out not long from now. Disgust and fascination mixed. The sweets well up inside him, and still he can't take his hand away. She won't let him anyway.

He doesn't like it when I eat chocolate, Miranda says.

She's there again the next day, and the next.

At weigh-in Sunday morning, it turns out Flipper's lost three pounds, champion of the week. His cabin gets pizza that night. He dares to dream about her. Special Dark, he's been saving them: three for her and three for him. Flipper will lie next to her in the grass, eyes closed, both of them. Lying alone on his hard little bunk, he can feel the morning sunlight on his skin, tickle of damp grass. With his eyes closed, Flipper sees the milk-white and porcelain-blue of her breasts, she's careless with them. Once he saw her right down to the nipple. Two bunks away, a boy is sobbing in the darkness. The wind is churning the leaves of the trees outside, a sound like rain. Right down to the nipple. He opens his eyes to the darkness of the cabin, and imagines that she meant for him to see her.

In the morning it is raining. Two days until it will end. He stays away from the tree, to save the last of the Special Dark. When the third day comes up sunny, he barely finishes his breakfast. Miranda has been with him each night, growing inside him. He has dared to dream about her.

At the tree he finds a litter of foil and wrappers on the ground, nothing in the hollow. Another camper has been here.

Flipper shrinks again, pathetic. A cheap sound like a crying baby doll bubbles out of his thick stupid body, and scalding tears. Flipper is the fattest and the stupidest. Miranda has big zits all over her face. He can't go see her empty-handed, but the camp store sells only wholesome snacks, nothing she would love, nothing for them to share. The nearest real chocolate is in the country store, three or four miles away, the rumor says. It might as well be Mercury. He can feel her in the sunlight, how she would turn her face toward the sun, eyes closed, like some vine twisting toward the light. Gone and gone. Flipper is discarded, weeping trash bag.

Now Flipper is hurrying down the shoulder of the road. Now Flipper is running. Big trucks are driving by, inches from his feet. It doesn't matter what happens to him.

For love, he thinks, oh love. The word comes into his mind at an angle, like another language, because it's the wrong word. What he really wants is this: He wants her to look up at him when he comes into the clearing, he wants her to see the big bar of chocolate in his hands, wants her to know that he had gone especially for her, all the way to the country store, way out in the forbidden world, the dangerous world, and brought this back for her. He wants to see her eat as much as she wants. He wants the smear of melted chocolate on her lips.

Hero.

Now Flipper is trying not to cry again. The counselors caught up to him while he was in the country store, or maybe the bitch behind the counter called the camp on him. She has a hatchet face: bitch. They joke back and forth. This isn't the first time. While she's laughing, Flipper backs up to the candy counter, slips a book-size slab of Special Dark into underwear. No one will notice. His shorts are enormous. He can feel the waxy wrapper, cool against the skin of his ass, and then it melts and shapes itself to him.

Kid Galahad, the counselor says, driving back. She sees the crafty look in his pig eyes.

He's grounded for a week, confined to cabin. His parents are written. He carefully straightens the bar of Special Dark back into a rectangle during the hot afternoons alone, in the sunlight next to his cot. He can feel her in the sunlight, how she would turn her face toward the sun, eyes closed, like some vine twisting toward the light. He can feel her inside him. He practices in whispers, moving his lips: I brought this for you. I got this at the country store.

Now Flipper is standing alone in the little clearing. The sound of an outboard motor rings up from the lake, splashing, swimming, aluminum canoes. She isn't there.

He'll come again tomorrow, and the day after. He will come every week for the rest of the summer but she will not be there. Miranda's gone to have her baby.

Flipper knows this right away. The clearing is empty. Flipper is a big stupid baby.

He lies on his side in the grass. He sees himself from above, like he was already dead. Trash bag. He puts his hand on the bare skin of his own soft stomach, remembering the tight-stretched skin under the thin cloth. He touches his tiny dick. He saw her once, right down to the nipple. He takes the chocolate bar out of the bag, unwraps the waxy paper and the foil, breaks off a little jagged triangle and slips it in his mouth, no hurry, he's got all afternoon, he's got the whole thing to himself. But the taste is wrong or the feel of it in his mouth, maybe from the melting and unmelting but it tastes like breakfast food or sawdust. She isn't coming. He eats the whole bar anyway, slowly, like it was his duty. Dust, sunlight, aluminum canoes, the grass against his neck. He finishes the chocolate and wads the wrapper up into a ball and stands up, a little dizzy from the sugar but the empty place inside him is still empty. He wants, he wants, he wants, an open mouth and nothing more. Flipper is still hungry.

Honeymoon

This is 1974, October: Jane and I are drinking our way home from the wedding, bar to bar down the Blackfoot River. Jane's girlfriend and mine, too, just married this third party, this knife-maker, up by Seeley Lake.

"This isn't going to make sense," I tell Jane. "We're not going to wake up some morning and this is all going to be clear."

Evening sunlight, leaves skittery across the blacktop. Jane's driving. She says, "It's not that complicated."

"What?"

"We've been jilted," Jane says.

"We could have taken better care of her."

"She's a *big girl*," Jane says. "She can take care of herself."

A silence, in which we see an apparition of the bride, floating above the highway in her mother's white lacy dress and a pair of Red Wing logger boots. The knife-maker wore his best buckskin. It was sunny but cold. Her parents looked on, like they had accidentally wandered into a nudist colony, trying not to stare at the small dirty cabin he had built, the wood chips and deerskins tanning in the wedding yard.

The bride invited only people she had slept with. We had already sorted this out.

"Bar," I tell Jane, and she steers the pickup into the parking lot. Everything else is four-wheel drive, enormous. A dead deer stares at us from the bed of the truck next to ours.

"Somebody got lucky," Jane says.

"What do you want? People around here kill deer."

"I didn't say anything," Jane says.

"There are more deer in North America now than there were when Columbus landed," I announce, and Jane looks at me.

~   ~   ~

Inside is men in camouflage, talk and cigarette smoke, shots taken and shots missed. Jane orders whiskey to go with her beer. A table in the corner is still in face paint, black and green.

"It smells in here," Jane says.

"It's this stuff," I tell her. "They wear it to disguise the human scent. It's supposed to smell like deer sex."

"This has been quite a day," she says, "so far." She downs the shot of bar bourbon in one take, and I admire the fine workings of her neck. Her blue work shirt is open two buttons. She's quite a beautiful girl, Jane is, despite the crew cut and the total lack of availability—about an inch taller than I am, with long arms and fingers, Connecticut money.

"Diamond earrings," I say.

"It was her *wedding*," Jane says. "I'm supposed to be *her friend*."

"Or something."

"Don't get snippy." She ran her finger around the rim of the empty shot glass. "You're going to have to drive, I think."

A rumble of laughter from the end of the bar—three bearded faces that look away when I look up, all but one who holds my eyes.

"I don't mind driving," I tell her. "What I don't feel like is criticism."

"I don't like this myself," she says. "Not much. Let's get something to go."

"We could just head back."

"Not yet. I mean, if you really want to . . ."

"No." I don't want to be back in my regular life just yet—the empty room, the roommates. We want something to happen. There's this silence between us—Jane, myself, our mutual friend—like static on a long-distance wire, looking for the right words to say to make everything better.

~　　~　　~

Jane buys: a twelve-pack of Lucky Lager and a double bourbon in a plastic go-cup. She's got a job on the railroad. I'm still in college, cleaning up Married Student Housing, living on peanut butter and Top Ramen. My turn to drive starts when we get out to the parking lot, where the dead deer is still staring at us. Jane can't seem to take her eyes off it.

"You get a pleasure out of that," she says.

"I don't know."

Windows open, we drive down to the fishing access area, then a couple of miles and down onto a gravel road. Jane's thinking. "I can imagine pulling the trigger," she says, when the truck stops. "That's not the problem. It's just that next thing, where you open them up, dump their guts out. Does that make sense to you?"

A breeze down the canyon blows the day right out of the air, and suddenly it's cold.

~　　~　　~

We get out, drape ourselves on the rocks, clutching cold beer cans in cold hands. She finished the whiskey on the ride down.

"I've never seen her look like that," Jane says. "When she was doing it, you know, up there with the J.P. and everybody looking at her. It's almost like she was happy."

"Look what I can do."

"That's right. Look how far I can go."

"And none of you can follow me," I say. The river is rushing over rocks, that same busy, blank sound: static. The sunlight has passed out of the canyon and the sky, through the trees overhead, is a delicate gray.

Jane takes another beer, hands me one, keeps her eyes to herself.

"I saw her like that once before," I tell Jane. "When I hitchhiked out to Iowa, last summer, they let me see her in the hospital."

"Don't pull rank on me," Jane says. "Your pain is worse than mine is, right?—no, that's not it. You've got a right to it. I'm just her fucking dyke girlfriend but you."

"I didn't mean that."

"You didn't have to mean that. You didn't have to *do* anything to have a right to her. You've got all of nature on your side. Fuck, I'm drunk."

"I'm sorry."

"Don't fucking be sorry," Jane says, standing up, walking in a small tight circle. "Don't listen to me. I'm just so fucking sad."

Now I'm pissed, my delicate feelings and so on, but there's nothing to say. She's gone, Jane's gone, I'm just sitting there.

"You pick the weak ones first," Jane says. "You pick the ones that are weak and sick, the ones that can't keep up with the others, right? It's just part of the process."

"Be quiet," I tell her, "please."

And she stops and I think that I am finally there, that I am present for her and she is paying attention and she will help me know what to feel about this.

~　　　~　　　~

But this is not the case. She's listening, and after a few seconds I hear it, too: a rustling in the dry leaves along the bank, snapping twigs and moving branches and then I am standing too, my beer spilling into the rocks and gravel, and I think *night, cold, forest* and tighten my belly against the danger.

A small deer trails out of the bushes, into the clearing along the bank, trailing a yellow arrow from its gut.

"Oh, Jesus," Jane says.

I back away. A wounded animal is dangerous, always. Blood runs down its hind leg into the rock as it looks from one of us to the other, dull eyes: We are part of some awful dream.

"Jesus Christ," Jane says. She kneels in the gravel, to make herself smaller, and starts to crawl toward the tiny deer.

"What are you doing?" I ask her.

The deer edges away, suddenly bright-eyed, endangered.

"You're scaring it," I tell her.

"It's the smell," Jane says. "He won't go anywhere near the smell. Don't let him get away."

Facing the wounded deer, she backs into the river, up to her thighs and then her waist and then, as she dips her body and her hair into the water, I think the river has carried her away. It hasn't. The deer and I watch, both wondering, as she appears from out of the water and then slowly, gently, up the bank toward the animal. It watches for as long as it can, then wheels and darts back into the bankside weeds.

"Get him," Jane says.

But I already have a heavy, jagged rock in my hand, I am already slogging through, the weed stems wrapping themselves around my legs and clouds of dry pollen in my face. The deer is nowhere. When I stop, though, I can hear him, twenty or thirty feet away, running. I run after him, but he quickly outdistances me. I stop again, and there is nothing: the silence of the river.

It's the last ten minutes before dark. The air is luminous gray.

Jane is freezing when I get back, I can see it in her face, and in the way she hunches over herself, shivering.

"What were you trying to do?" she asks. I still seem to have the rock in my hand.

I let it drop to the ground. "Nothing," I tell her.

"You were going to kill it."

"It was already dead, good as dead. Not with that arrow in its side."

"I know," she says. "I'm cold."

~　　~　　~

Jane has a sleeping bag in her truck, behind the seat, she tells me, next to the flares and the flashlight. "Hurry," she says, "I'm freezing."

It's dark. I don't know how dark it is until I open the door of the truck, and the dome light goes on and it's bright as a living room. I find the sleeping bag where she said it was, but when I close the door again, I can't see anything.

"Did you see a deer?" asks a man's voice, close up.

"Fuck," I say, and jump back. "I didn't even see you."

It's the hunter, carrying his big machine of a bow. His face is camouflage. "I've been tracking it since two o'clock," he says.

"We saw it but it's gone."

The hunter slumps against the steel back bumper of the truck. "I've been tracking that deer all day, my son and I. I thought he had a good clean shot."

"It's not your son's fault," I tell him.

"He gut-shot the fucking thing," the hunter says. "I'm sorry, but he was twenty feet away! Gut-shot it."

"I've got to go," I tell him, and head down to the river, trailing the sleeping bag like laundry behind me. *It's not your son's fault* rings in my ears. I hope Jane didn't hear me.

"I'm freezing," she says. "I've got to get out of these clothes."

"Just go up to the truck."

"I don't know," she says, and in the flashlight circle I can see that she's blue and shivering: *night, cold, forest.* "I'm OK," she says. "I'm just . . ."

The sleeping bag is the Boy Scout kind, big and square with duck-print flannel inside. I zip it open, lay it on the ground, she strips at the edge of the flashlight beam and huddles into it. Her clothes lie in a cold wet puddle beside her head.

"I'm sorry," Jane says.

"No, you're right."

"I . . ."

"Don't worry about it."

"No, it's just, I don't know—me and me and me, you know? My suffering."

"Don't worry about it," I tell her, in my best John Wayne. I get up to where the twelve-pack is lying on its side in the sand, a souvenir of some earlier lifetime. The beer is cold as the air, cold as the water.

"Could I have a sip of that, please?" Jane asks.

"Are you all right?"

"I'll be fine in a minute."

I sit in the sand again, lean my back against a damp log, the cold damp temperature of night. I take Jane's head onto my lap, feeling the cold stiff bristles of her crew cut, and bring the can to her lips like she is an invalid; like I am nursing her, taking care.

"Another, please," Jane says, and I give her another. We finish the first one, another and another, I can feel the trembling has quieted down. I can see the edge of the moon crawling into the canyon. She's fine. I'm fine, though I don't see how we are going to go anywhere from here. I'm still holding her head in my lap, her fine-boned head.

"Are you drunk?" she asks me, and I nod sure. "Are you too drunk to make the drive home?"

"I don't know. I hope I'm OK."

"You think I'm drunk enough to sleep with you?"

"I don't know," I say. "I don't think so."

"You think I'm lonely enough?"

I don't say anything. The river runs by us, the wind in the trees. She leans her head against my chest and stares up into the sky.

"Orion," she says.

Carolina Beach

The Christian puppet show is closed up and gone for the winter, or maybe for good. The peeling backdrops—a desert, a house, a mountain—have been left out in the rain, in front of an audience of empty benches.

Vincent and Laurie walk slowly along the boardwalk. The two of them and the gulls and nobody. The boardwalk spans the dunes between the town and the Atlantic; on the one side spray and foam and thunder, on the other side concrete, painted tropical blue and pink. The distant bells and clatter of coin-operated fun.

Vincent is holding her hand in the pocket of his parka, for the first time. Her hand is small and cold and full of bones. The salt air is too chilly for Vincent to be sweating, but he is sweating anyway in his pile and Gore-Tex. All this black nylon, he thinks. He must look like a refugee from a SWAT team. Laurie wears a red bandanna on her head, which is wet with the rain and blowing spray by now. The wet cotton sticks to her head, which is completely bald. Her *skull*, Vincent thinks. He can't help himself. She's wearing a short studded-leather jacket, a biker jacket, which is not really her personality. In fact she has a home in Cary, two children, a Windstar minivan. But people stare at bald women.

"At least this way they don't feel sorry for me," she says to Vincent, lighting a joint.

He looks away at the ocean, trying to keep from getting caught. He feels sorry for her, himself.

"Besides I'm getting to like it," Laurie says. "Being visible. I take the kids down to Winn-Dixie, and it's like an event. I feel dangerous."

Vincent looks down at the joint in his hand, like it just appeared there by itself. He tries to hand it back to her.

"I'm really not supposed to," he says. "I'm an officer of the court."

"You're just a regular lawyer," Laurie says. "I know what that means. Besides, I've got a note from my doctor. It's practically legal."

Vincent still doesn't want to—he hasn't smoked marijuana

in twenty years—but she seems to want him to, so he takes a hit: the familiar, nostalgic smoke. This was college.

"Do you want to go back?" he asks.

"A little farther," Laurie says. "The air—I just like the air."

An hour ago, back in the hotel, she had thrown up at the smell of the room: deodorizer, stale smoke, popcorn butter drifting up from the arcades.

"Let's try for the gazebo," she says. It's the farthest point out, a little spur of the boardwalk toward the ocean, fifty yards out, and then a little covered room where surfers gather in warm weather. What if she can't make it all the way back? Vincent pictures himself trying to carry her and knows that her small bones would break if he tried to pick her up. I am clumsy, he thinks, clumsy.

But he could bring the car around. She could wait in the shelter. Really, there's no danger.

"Look," she says, and points to a black something in the trough of the waves. There's water on his glasses and Vincent can barely see. At first he thinks it must be a drowned man, a body floating, and he gets the thrill of danger down in his stomach. Then he sees it's a surfer, after all, a boy in a black wetsuit.

"This is when you get the big water," Vincent says. "Most days, there's nothing to it."

"You know how to surf?"

Vincent looks down at himself, the swell of his belly under the parka, and laughs.

"I'd break the board in two if I tried it now," he says.

"I used to, though. We used to come down to Wrightsville every weekend, all the way from Chapel Hill. About a four-hour drive, before they built the interstate. I had a Volkswagen bus with a bed in the back."

"What was that for?"

"You could guess," Vincent says.

"I bet you were beautiful then," she says. "Surfer boy. I bet you were skinny and tan and I bet you had one of those grooves running down your spine, that little soft groove. Women *look* at men, did you know that?"

"In theory."

"I'm giving away all the secrets," Laurie says. "Anything you want to know."

"It's a little late for me," he says, walking her along.

At last they reach the end of the boardwalk, into the half-shelter of the cedar roof. The sides are open, though, and the wind whips through. She won't let go of his hand. She pulls him down to sit next to her on the bench, a wall behind them to break the wind, and she takes the wet, extinguished joint from his other hand and still she won't let go of his hand, there in his pocket. Suddenly Vincent knows her body is there next to his, under the leather and the sweater and the jeans. Laurie's wearing her fake breasts today. Some days she doesn't.

"I bet you were beautiful," Laurie says again. "Surfer boy."

Before she can talk anymore, before she can light the joint, he reaches over and kisses her for the first time. Somehow he manages to surprise himself, even. He is sure and calm and easy with her.

He kisses her face and her neck and he pulls her body over his, huddled out of the wind. She is so light! She kneels over him like a child, her face floating above his, and Vincent presses his cheek into the buckle of her motorcycle jacket.

"I was hoping you would do that," Laurie says.

His heart is beating fast inside him like a child's heart, quick and fluttery. He doesn't know what to do with his hands. Beneath the leather, under his cheek, is the soft spring of her prosthetic breast, and under that is the scar, which he has never seen. Today or tonight he will look at the scar. He *knows* this, all of a sudden, and it sends a panic through him, a physical panic that starts in his spine and ends at the root of his testicles. This woman is full of illness and death.

It shames him to think such a thing but there it is.

He looks into her face, and sees that she has gone gray and empty. Quickly she peels herself off him, goes and stands at the empty doorway of the gazebo. She doubles her arms against her belly and presses them in. All Vincent can see is her small back, doubled over. He could never cross the few feet between them. She's gone.

Then, after a minute, the attack passes.

"I always wreck things," Laurie says.

"Don't start talking," Vincent says.

Vincent moves up behind her, arms around her belly, the wind in their faces. The leather, the cloth, the skin, the scar, he thinks. He can't help himself. Still, there she is: Laurie.

~   ~   ~

They met in poetry class, of all places, a dingy little basement room in the Durham Public Library. Vincent signed up for reasons that are still unclear to him: something about turning forty-five, something about reading the word *bachelor* in a magazine. He had been divorced for eight years and had lately taken to cooking gourmet dinners for himself.

He knew from the first that the poetry class was a mistake: terrifying retired nurses and sensitive bikers, a multipierced lesbian—a graduate student from somewhere—for a teacher. It was awful, the things they wrote about: suicide attempts and rapes and so on. Either that or the opposite, "To A Friend" and "Kitty's Playtime." Most of the class was continuing on from the semester before Christmas, and the graduate student was fed up with all of them, every one except Laurie, in her leather jacket. Vincent thought they were lovers at first. He sat through the first class, and the second and third—it was too late for a refund—staring at the plain outline of the teacher's nipple ring through her T-shirt and wondering what was on television at that moment.

In the third class, though, it was Laurie's turn, and she read five or six little poems she called "Chemotherapy Haiku." Vincent can almost remember: Puking in cook pot, something something something cherry blossom. Rain against the glass. She read them out loud in a small certain voice and gradually Vincent figured out what was going on: illness and plain speaking. He suspected the poems weren't any good—he'd taken a creative-writing course or two in college, to improve his verbal skills for law school—but it didn't matter. She stood in a spotlight of her own making and spoke directly to each of them. When she finished, there was a silence so long and awful that Vincent just wanted to slip out of the room and have a drink. The teacher was weeping when she looked up. So, she said with a breaking voice. Anybody?

Vincent was undermined completely by this outburst of feeling. It felt like something big that had happened to him a long time ago, not quite remembered, was starting to happen again, some deep underground force like the movements of the tides. . . .

He didn't say a word for the rest of the class but then, somehow, found the nerve to ask her out for coffee afterward. She couldn't—a problem with the baby-sitter—and then the next week she was absent, and Vincent worried about her. But then the week after that, she was standing in front of him at the end of class—half his size!—saying, If you still want to . . . , and they ended up at the coffee department of the new Harris-Teeter, a supermarket the size of a small town, with a florist and a fishmonger and an espresso bar.

He was a lawyer, she was a car-dealership finance person, one shade off crooked. There was never anybody in the coffee place but Vincent and Laurie and, once or twice, the teacher, whose name was Nix. Laurie was more lively and animated with Nix than she was with Vincent, which was a disappointment. She would say things to Nix that she wouldn't say to him. Once, talking about her ex, she said, "You don't stay married to a car salesman for twelve years and not learn how to give a blow job."

And that's how I got here, Vincent thinks, fighting the wind back through the beach town, going to fetch the car. He left her back in the gazebo. He walks quickly back through the center of town: cold, abandoned in this weather. The Skee-Ball arcades are almost empty but still alive with noise. It seems odd that these few teenagers could put up this much of a racket. Half the stores are boarded up, the bars are deserted, the windows fogged with condensation, the ocean roaring and the ocean wind and Laurie alone out on the edge. He left her there.

She kissed me, Vincent thinks. She actually kissed me.

The center of town smells strongly of french-fry grease and hot dogs. The smell of the food makes Vincent realize that he is hungry. He shouldn't be, though he hasn't eaten since breakfast. He should be faithful to her. Laurie eats crackers, clear soups, Popsicles, plain yogurt. But Vincent can't help himself. He stops at a pizza-by-the-slice place—still strangely open, this late in the season—and orders a slice of pepperoni. He waits for it to heat, while Laurie waits for him in the gazebo, alone. He wolfs the pizza as he walks toward the hotel.

"What took you?" Laurie says when he pulls up in the Mercedes. She's still tired.

"It took a while to walk," he says, "all the way back through town."

But then it seems completely pointless to lie to her.

"I stopped for a second and got something to eat," he says.

Laurie settles into the firm leatherette of her seat and sighs with pleasure: rest.

"Good for you," she says. "You take care of yourself."

Vincent watches the single big wiper sweep across the glass for a second: the impressionist smear of the beach town in the rain, pink, blue, orange. She's all outside, now, brittle and hard to the touch.

"I didn't mean to leave you stranded," he says.

"But I mean it," Laurie says. "I'm worried about you."

"I'm all right."

"I didn't ask for this," Laurie says. "This just *happened* to me. But you—you're walking into trouble with your eyes wide open. You could get hurt, Vincent."

Vincent reaches over the gearshift knob and kisses her wet scarf, the bare skin of her skull under it. He waits for her to turn her face to him, to be kissed again, but she doesn't.

"The day I met you was a lucky day," he says, as plainly as he can, not trying to sell her. "I'm lucky to know you."

"Don't be an asshole, Vincent. Don't try to make me cry."

"I'm not," he says.

"I'm not going to make it, Vincent," she says. "This is not going to be fine."

"You don't know," he says.

"That's right," she says. "You don't know either. Nobody knows. It's just a number, fifty percent."

Vincent is shocked to hear the number. She has never told him before. His heart pulls toward her, there in his chest. He wants to hold her, protect her.

But Laurie sees him surprised. She sees the pity. She shakes her head softly, sits upright in her seat.

There's nothing more for him to say. He slips the car into

first and crawls off toward the hotel again, a cloud of diesel smoke behind him, faces in the side windows like white blurs, and Laurie, silent, beside him.

~   ~   ~

Laurie needs to take a nap. Downstairs in the bar, a baseball game is going on the TV and the ocean is whipping and waving and pounding in the wind outside the big picture windows. It's almost empty, just Vincent, the bartender, and a table full of college boys with backward hats.

He orders a beer and tries to enjoy the game: the Braves and the Padres, live in the Atlanta sunshine. Not far from here, Vincent thinks, looking out at the rain. He could be in that sunshine. Maybe Laurie is right, maybe he wants to suffer; except he doesn't. He pretends to watch the ball game while he examines himself, and as far as he can tell, there's no part of him that wants to suffer. He wants to kiss Laurie and talk with her and hold her hand. The simplicity of his desires.

No, he corrects himself. Not that simple.

Maybe it's the dope he smoked with her, but he can't keep his eyes on the television set. He can't quite follow the thread. He keeps drifting out to the wind and rain and ocean outside, the wild spray off the tops of the waves. He sips his beer—there's no hurry—but when he's done, he puts on his parka again and raises the hood and leaves the rest of them there in the smoke and TV sound. The wind outside is clean and saline, purifying. The waves are pounding the sand.

He leaves his brown shoes in the deserted patio of the bar

and steps barefoot out across the wet sand. After a few feet, he stops to roll his pant legs up, to keep the sand out of them. He's out in wild nature now. That's what he feels like anyway: the miles without end of heaving, pounding water, the kingdoms of fish down below, forests of seaweed, sharks and marlin and gray whales. He feels himself drawn down to the edge of the water. He walks along where the cold seawater laps over his feet with every advancing wave, the white, lacy outwash. Down where you are going, Vincent thinks. Not that Laurie will die, not necessarily. Just that this is what will make the decision, the blind forces, wind and water. Not Laurie's wishes, not his own. Not her life or her desires or her goodness or the mistakes she might have made, none of this will make any difference. He thinks of waiting for her in the street outside her ex-husband's house, waiting while she dropped her boys off so she could leave with him for this weekend. They were already late. She didn't invite him in with her, and it took her almost twenty minutes to come out again.

Her face was set and angry, coming down the walk. She didn't say anything until they were well on the freeway.

"It just kills me," she finally said.

"What?"

"The idea of that asshole and his asshole wife with my kids."

She let it rest for another seven or eight miles, then gave a tight little laugh and patted him on the hand.

"I'm sorry," she said. "It just drives me crazy, you know?"

"I bet," Vincent said.

Laurie said, "It's enough to make you want to live."

~   ~   ~

"I'll tell you something," Laurie says. She's still stretched out on her bed, after the nap, but she's better—her face has some color to it, her eyes some of their snap and sparkle. She's wearing an REM concert T-shirt, way oversized, and a new blue bandanna. She says, "This afternoon? Out on the beach? You know, you were talking all that stuff about how you used to come down here from college. And I was thinking, Jesus Christ—when you were down here at the beach with your friends, out having a time, I was up at Camp Lejeune. And I was eighteen years old and Tyler was running around in diapers and I was already pregnant with Livvie, and I used to come down to Wrightsville sometimes, you know. Dragging Ty down the beach, hoping he didn't shit in the sand, me swollen up like a cow. People would look at me, you know. They used to feel sorry for me, I could see it in their eyes. And I hated that. That's why I was so mad at you."

After a minute, Vincent says, "I didn't even know you were mad at me."

She stretches her hand across the bedspread—the scratchy hotel fabric, whatever space-age material they use—and takes Vincent's hand, and their hands lie on the coverlet.

~   ~   ~

Vincent makes dinner in his room—it's the one reason he brought them to this hotel, the little ship's kitchen in the corner of the room, a two-burner stove and a wet bar. He has brought, from home, a French enameled chicken fryer, a seventy-dollar pepper mill, kosher salt, fresh basil, cheese from Italy, and California olive oil. When the water for the pasta is finally boiling—the stove is weak—he pours the olive oil into the heated pan and stirs in the minced garlic and the room fills with the smell. Vincent closes his eyes to smell it better.

"Is that some garlic?" Laurie yells through the connecting door. "Man, open the window or something."

"Is it bothering you?"

"Not at the moment," she says, "but you can never tell."

Quickly—the garlic is browning nicely—he hurries across the room and slides the big glass door open all the way. They're on the fifth floor but still the sound of the surf fills the room, and the smell of salt water. Before the garlic can burn, he pours a quart of diced fresh tomatoes into the pan, tomatoes from his garden, then salt and pepper and that's all. "Dinnertime," he calls to Laurie, rushing to drain the pasta before it loses its bite. While the last of the water is draining, he stirs a handful of fresh basil leaves into the tomatoes, then another, a shake of pepper. Perfect.

"Dinner," he says again, to the blank face of the connecting door.

Nothing.

She won't be a minute, he thinks. He pours the pasta and the sauce together in a stoneware bowl, a bit more pepper, a double handful of the Reggiano and stirs it all up. Hot and perfect.

"Laurie?" he calls out. "Laurie? Are you OK?"

"You go ahead," she says.

"What's the matter?"

"I'm OK," she says. "You go ahead and eat."

"I'll wait a minute," Vincent says.

"You go ahead," she says.

Vincent looks at the steaming bowl and he is instantly, unreasonably angry. All his time and care and planning and she can't even do him this one small courtesy. Suddenly he's tired of taking care of her, waiting on her, putting up with the thousand small discomforts of a day with Laurie. He wants to pick the bowl up and throw it against the wall, he can see it, the red sauce and the green leaves of the basil lying in a heap on the hotel carpeting, the steam and mess and fuck you, anyway, Laurie. . . .

And just as quickly it passes. However tired of Laurie's illness he is, Laurie is a hundred times more. Vincent knows this. He is just selfish.

He goes to the open balcony door and presses his forehead against the glass, cool on his hot skin. Close to tears, he thinks. I haven't been this close in years.

Then, after a minute, Vincent sits at the table, alone. He opens the good bottle of wine he brought for them and pours himself a glass, and then one for Laurie, for Laurie's empty place. He serves himself a plate of the pasta, which is not as good now as it had been a minute ago, when it was fresh and hot, but still edible. He wonders if this is how it's going to be, Vincent at the table with his own thoughts: one knife, one fork, one glass, one plate.

~ ~ ~

Then he is standing outside her door, in the hall, a wineglass in each hand. He feels like a suitor. He feels like he should have some small handful of flowers, a what? a nosegay, he remembers. What a word.

"Who is it?" Laurie calls.

"It's me," Vincent says.

In a slow minute—the time it takes for her to get from the bed to the door—she lets him in.

"What are you doing out there?" she asks.

"Oh," he says, "I didn't want to let the smell in, you know, the food. I thought you might not like it."

"Oh, Christ," she says. She turns her back on him and walks away, leaving Vincent to decide what to do with the open door. He sets the wineglasses down and closes it, follows her back to the bed, where she sits on the edge.

"What?" he asks.

"You need to take care of yourself," she says. "You need to, Vincent. I'm sorry, I don't mean to tell you what to do."

"OK," Vincent says. He takes a deep breath, goes over to the window and looks outside: the neon pink-and-green of the boardwalk ends all at once, and beyond that—out in the immense black nothing of the ocean—a few white puffy clouds are scattered. He presses his cheek against the cool glass. He closes his eyes. When he opens them again, he can see her on the bed, reflected in the dark glass of the door: slight, tired. She's wearing jeans, a sleeveless shirt, a perky little wig that makes her look like Pat Benatar.

"Let's start this over," Vincent says.

He turns the overhead light off, the one that makes this place look bright as an operating room. He shuts off the pendulum light over the table, he turns the bedside lamps off, one side then the other. In the half-lit glow that follows, Laurie looks plausible, desirable. Almost a regular woman. She looks confused.

"Have you got a joint?" Vincent asks her.

She shrugs her shoulders: sure.

"Let's go out on the balcony," he says. "If you're up for it. I don't want the hotel cops to come sniffing under the door."

"Sure," she says, "whatever."

She piles into a sweatshirt, follows him out onto the cement porch. It's cold, too cold for Laurie. The afternoon's rain lingers as damp in the air. Laurie lights the reefer and passes it to Vincent, in silence. Reefer, Vincent thinks. Hooter. What do they call them these days?

The red wine tastes better and better, the stars pass by in a disorderly spray. Laurie sits there, in a white webbing chair, all knotted up in herself.

"Tell me what I'm doing," he says.

She shakes her head.

"Tell me what you want me to do."

"I don't want you to do anything," she says. "This isn't your fault. I just can't, is all. If this was any other time, anyplace else in my life, I would be so happy to . . ."

"It's just an experiment," Vincent says.

"What?"

He looks at her and sees that, even if he felt like it,

he couldn't make words out of what he's feeling. Down at the center is some simplicity. He reaches his hand out and takes hers and Laurie doesn't pull away. Her hand is cold and small and full of bones but Vincent can warm it between his big hot clumsy hands, and he does. The blood under the skin, he thinks.

"Let's go inside," he says.

"Look, Vincent . . ."

"Please," he says.

In the slanting light of the window he can see her face, and she is angry with him, the invader. And Vincent knows exactly why: Her body, her children, her idea about the future, Vincent is asking her to feel them again. He knows it's a lot. He knows he wouldn't give it, if he was her.

But Laurie rises, turns her face from him and leads him into the room again. She leads him to the bed and then leaves him there, sitting on the edge of the rumpled covers while she turns the rest of the lights off and draws the curtains closed. He thinks that he will see her scars next. He wishes he could see her face, read it. He feels the thrill of fear again, down at the root of his testicles: the damaged woman, the nearness of injury and death.

"I'll be there in a second," Laurie says—like a wife, he thinks, exactly like a wife—and disappears into the bathroom.

Vincent sits there, lump on a log.

But this is what he asked her for. He was the one that asked. Vincent doesn't know if he has the nerve to go through with this but he must act as if he knows. A lesson he has learned from his life as a man. He unties his shoes, there in the dark, and stuffs his socks in them and arranges them under the bed, neatly. He feels for the chair in the dark, drapes his shirt over the back, folds his pants and underwear on the seat. His own fat body. He sits on the edge of the bed, waiting. He lies down, experimentally, then sits back up again. He thinks about what her scars will look like, what they will feel like. He never once— give him this—he never wishes that he had not come.

Red Dress

I wanted to be a mixologist. I don't know where I got the desire, or even the word, which still has a kind of magic for me: mixologist. In the syllables of those letters are my parents' parties, nights of smoke and laughter and lipstick. I borrowed the Mr. Boston bartender's guide from the liquor cabinet and read it in my bed, imagining myself pouring, shaking, stirring, holding the sugar cube in a slotted spoon and drizzling the red liquor through. I learned the difference between lemon zest and lemon peel, I memorized the steps for a perfect Ramos Gin Fizz, I knew how to pour a Manhattan, a Stinger, a Grasshopper, a White Russian.

My sister was gone to college by then, and our only television was downstairs. On party nights, I could neither sleep nor read; I lay on my bed with the light on and listened to the undifferentiated oceanic hubbub below, louder as the night went on, the whole house gradually filling with cigarette smoke. Occasionally a guest, a man trying to find the upstairs bathroom, would come through the door of my room and find me on the bed, awake—which seemed to come not only as a surprise but as an embarrassment to him, as if he had caught me at some shameful act. He would shut the light off on the way out.

Other nights I would sit in the dark at the top of the stairs and listen. I would try to imagine myself among the guests, try to imagine what they were talking about. I could hear my mother's high-pitched, brittle laughter, imagine her mixing and drifting from guest to guest in her red party dress. I didn't want to be one of them; I just wanted to know what made them so loud and excited, what they were hoping for.

I promoted myself to doorman at some point. My job was to answer the bell, greet the guests, take their coats and point them toward the bar. It's always winter, the way I remember it. I think now that it might have been just one year, one winter giving way to spring and summer, but I remember it as always, world without end. This job as doorman was unsatisfying. I was closer to the action, but I was visible. I was always being called by the doorbell just as the conversation was becoming interesting, just as they were starting to forget that I was among them; or coming back after the punch line, the joke I was too young to hear, the women still giggling. They couldn't help themselves. Or else, as I drifted or sidled to the edge of the group, I would be noticed, I would be called attention to with a greeting or a wave of a cigarette, and the talk would instantly turn toward the innocuous—the lives of pets, movies that had been seen, *West Side Story* or *Doctor Zhivago*. My parents' life and the lives of their friends seemed even more jumbled and fragmentary than they had before.

My mother, for instance. In everyday life, she was vague, sometimes absentminded, wandering the house while my father was at work like she was half asleep. In my dreams, I see her standing in an almost dowdy, unrevealing floral dress, an I-Love-Lucy dress, standing just inside the doorway of her bedroom, pausing, with one hand on the dresser, and trying to remember—you could see it in her face—what she had wanted from there. Was it laundry? Jewelry? Was she going out or staying in? I still don't know what she was actually thinking about, or dreaming about.

When she put on her red dress and her lipstick and descended into a party, though, she became an altogether different person—energetic, intense, almost uncomfortably alive. She was everywhere at once, laughing at jokes, holding her white cigarettes to be lit, carrying trays of olives and crackers and little squares of cheese on toothpicks. When someone spoke, especially if they were talking lightly or playfully, she was lit with concentration, her mouth moving into a half-smile or a half-frown as each new sentence came spilling out. Her attention was as urgent and narrow as a flashlight beam. Yours was the one face in the world, the one joke, the only scandalous story or amusing anecdote. She lit her subjects, one by one, and then moved on, and on.

Never to me. The one place her attention never lit was on my face; and if, sometime after eleven, she happened to notice that I was still awake—watching her, as ever, from my station by the door—all the old puzzlement would return to her face, and she would stare at me, wondering who I was and how I had gotten there, for a long moment before ordering me off to bed.

In her red party dress, she would tuck me into the sheets and she would kiss me good night and then leave, down the hall in a rustle of fabric. I would lie on my bed with the door open, drifting in and out of sleep, awakening to singing, to arguments and fights, sleeping again to dream of flowers and smoke, the laughter penetrating the thin screen of my sleep. Once I came to the top of the stairs, awake or nearly awake, in time to watch two men carry another out into the snow, a trickle of blood at the corner of his mouth. Once I heard somebody singing "Mairzy Doats," which I recognized from an old cartoon. Always the sound of my mother's laughter.

In the morning, before my parents woke up, which was never before ten-thirty or eleven, the house was mine: the ashtray-smell of dead cigarettes, lipsticky glasses, the toothpicks with their frilly cellophane tops scattered at random on the tablecloth. Only the flowers, the flowers that my mother and I had picked out so carefully the day before, had managed to stay fresh. I would wander barefoot through the wreckage, sniffing the half-finished drinks, the bourbon smell of my father in each of them, and having little conversations. I was winning. I was charming. I left laughter behind me wherever I went.

~　　~　　~

Sometime in spring, I was promoted to bartender. Not without an argument, though—my mother roused herself into one of her fits of motherhood, which were always a little imaginary, hypothetical. She was acting as if she were my mother, as if I were her son.

"I don't think he needs to stay up that late," she said.

This was the eve of another party—I can't understand how they could have had so many parties; it must have been two or three or four years altogether, not just one. My father, with my help, was setting up the drinks table, watching me carefully prepare the bowl of lime wedges, arrange the ice and shakers and Angostura bitters.

"He likes it," my father said. "Besides, he's always up till the wee small hours anyway."

"I always send him to bed."

"Doesn't mean he goes to sleep," my father said, turning his attention on me. "What do you do up there, anyway, champ? You aren't sleeping, are you?"

I didn't know how to respond to this. I didn't know what this was code for, or what the secret response might be.

"I never could stand to be left out myself," he said.

"Could I talk to you for a moment?" my mother asked.

They disappeared into the kitchen, leaving me to bustle, straighten and cut, laying out ashtrays, putting the glasses in an accurate row: wineglasses, cocktail glasses, highballs. If I could make myself indispensable, they would have to let me stay. The pleasure that I found in this kind of work—tidying, straightening, fussing—was intense, illicit. I straightened the flowers in their vases until they looked attractive from every angle. I placed ashtrays, coasters, bowls of pretzels and mixed nuts while my parents were arguing in the kitchen. My father would win eventually, as he did. He would wear her down like water. I took uneasy pleasure in knowing that he would prevail, knowing that I was fooling him. He thought I was pretending to be the little man.

Her face, when they came out of the kitchen, had a mixed, unsettled, lost look that made me feel lost with her. She was right and it didn't matter.

"You're on, champ," said my father. "Let's see if we can find you a necktie."

"Just until ten-thirty, though," my mother said.

"Ten-thirty or eleven," said my father. "We'll see how it's going."

She looked at him helplessly. He shouldn't have contradicted her in front of me, but she could do nothing about it. And then she looked at me, and it was strange; it felt like she could really see me, like the fog had cleared away momentarily and she recognized something, realized something.

"You be careful," she said to me.

"What does that mean?" my father asked her. "He's in his own living room, for Christ's sake. What could go wrong?"

She didn't answer for a moment; abstract, musing, she stared into my eyes, wondering what she saw there. I didn't know myself. I knew it was guilty, I knew it was something to hide, but I didn't know what its name was.

"He could cut himself," she said, turning away from my face, back to my father. "That's all I meant."

"He's not going to cut himself," said my father; though I did, in fact, slice my finger wide open with a paring knife while cutting up a second batch of limes at almost midnight.

Sixty or seventy men and women milled and perched and chatted in the first floor of the old house that night, a few of the men—hardy souls in wool sport jackets—out on the patio smoking cigarettes, a group around the stereo listening, I remember distinctly, listening to Olatunji and His Drums of Passion. The night had gone quickly, up until then. It amused them all to treat me as a genuine bartender, to make jokes about stiff ones and wet ones that I didn't quite understand—though I laughed eagerly—and to stuff dollar bills and loose silver into the jar that my father had insisted I put on the table in front of me. I had the glassware and the bottles and the mixers and the utensils all neatly aligned, near at hand. I wore a dish towel around my waist, as a sort of apron, to tidy up any spills; and I thought that I had fulfilled my duties as well as any grown-up bartender could, that I had been crisp and professional and nearly invisible, and I was proud of myself.

All of this changed in the course of one second. I was

cutting a lime and something—a shout, a burst of laughter—distracted my attention. When I looked down again, I saw that I had cut myself, and cut myself badly—that moment before the blood begins to flow, before anything starts to hurt, when the cut flap of skin turns white. I was immediately filled with shame. Quickly, before any of them could see me, I wrapped the cut finger in three or four thicknesses of cocktail napkin and slipped away from my post, through the kitchen and up the back stairs to the third, hard-to-find bathroom in the old part of the house.

I sat on the edge of the toilet and gingerly unwrapped the napkins. Blood seeped eagerly from the cut. In the bright, pale-green florescent light, the hand looked disembodied, already dead. I thought that if I lifted up the flap of skin I might see all the way to the bone; but I was already a little dizzy, a little queasy, so I didn't. What if I died there? What if I bled to death while the party raged downstairs?

But I wasn't going to die. I was going to get caught. I had overstepped myself, had pretended to be what I was not: competent, reliable, safe. In fact I was just a child, pretending.

I cut the light so that nobody would find me, and waited for the bleeding to subside. Clear moonlight came through the window, through the leafless trees outside. Stupid boy, I thought, stupid boy. Soon I would have to face them, and they would all know. The bleeding continued, slower and slower. I soaked the blood up with toilet paper. It hurt, by then, considerably, and I had to bend and unbend my finger several times to convince myself that I had not severed something vital.

After a few minutes, the blood slowed to a manageable trickle. In the moonlight—my eyes had adjusted perfectly well—I found gauze and adhesive tape in the medicine cabinet over the sink. Clumsy, single-handed, I wrapped the wound in bandages, finishing off with a pair of flesh-colored Band-Aids, in the hope I would not be discovered; in the hope that I could return to my post behind the bar. I hid the bloody paper under a magazine artfully placed over the top of the trash basket, slipped the lock, and went out into the hallway.

There in in the moonlight was my mother with a man: Kendellan, my father's college friend. They weren't touching, but something about their bodies alerted me, awkward, like frozen bodies in a game of freeze tag. Something had been started, interrupted. They must have been kissing—that blank unseeing look on her face that only slowly cleared, the flush on her neck—but I didn't know that then. I was an unwelcome surprise. Apart from that, nothing was clear.

"Ray," she said, "what are you doing up here?"

I held my injured hand behind my back, as casually as I could.

"Nothing," I said. And then, when I realized this didn't make any sense, I said, "The other bathrooms were all full."

"It's late, sweetie," she said, stepping away from Kendellan, who wouldn't give me his face. She bent toward me and I smelled her perfume. "It's late. Off we go. Let's go."

She took my hand—the innocent hand—and led me down the back hallway to my bedroom. The ebb and surge of conversation spilled up the stairs, but it was not for me, not that night. She led me to my door and kissed me briefly, dryly on the top of my head, as she had for most of my life, an assertion of normalcy, a statement that everything was, after all, in the right place, where it had been before.

She was wearing the red dress, same as always.

Then she turned, and closed the door, and went back to wherever she was going, leaving me, again, alone in my room. And maybe she was right—maybe I was overtired; maybe it was not right for me to be up so late—because when I caught sight of myself in the mirror, my crisp white shirt and real bow tie that my father had tied for me, it struck me as awful, and wrong, and unfair, and I didn't even have a name for it. I curled into a ball on my bed and cried, until I fell asleep in my clothes.

~   ~   ~

The finger became infected in the following days. I concealed it from my mother as long as I could, as the swelling grew and the pain drummed along with every beat of my heart; I didn't know exactly where I stood with her, I didn't want any new event between us until the old one had subsided. Kendellan and my mother, my mother and Kendellan, like something out of a dream—and in fact I did see the moment replayed in dreams, with photographic literalness; and I nearly managed to convince myself that it had never happened. If anything had happened at all.

By midweek, though, I had to do something. I couldn't sleep, and strange colors were appearing around the swollen cut. Awake, asleep, I felt like I was half body and half finger, every part of me focused on this one throbbing spot.

I confessed; I was examined, taken to the doctor, pronounced purulent. The cut was drained and cleaned and freshly bandaged. I was put on antibiotics and ordered to stay home for the rest of the week. I may have been seriously ill— I felt a kind of pleasant haze or fog in the edges of my vision, and the doctor and my mother were worried. It was in their faces. The gifted child does not miss this kind of thing.

Home, then, and a short week of television-watching, soup and crackers, the sound of the washing machine, and the hot breath of the dryer. I was special, once again. This should have been perfect; home alone, my mother and I, the chance to see the daily life she led, the life that was hidden while I was at school. I don't think I was sick any more than the next child, but I did enjoy being sick more than most of them. But this week was different; in the afterimage of that party—the dream of Mr. Kendellan, the interrupted moment—I felt like I was always on the verge of a question, I had to hold it back, a box I knew I didn't want to open. And my mother, when she saw me at all, seemed always about to launch into some new explanation. We were not easy with each other.

So I slept, and I read, and I slept some more, and I waited for the weekend, and after the weekend I would be back at school.

On Friday, though, I woke from my nap midway through the afternoon and my mother was gone—shopping, I thought, dry cleaning, general errands. Nothing was planned for the weekend, no flowers or special foods, no trips to the liquor store and hundred-dollar bills. My sister was coming home that evening. All the pieces of my world were in place. I went to my parents' bedroom, overlooking the street, and I looked out on the place where her car had been, the outline of her car in dry pavement on the rain-darkened street. It was three or three-thirty, overcast and dark. The light in the room was dim and gray, softshadowed, a delicate touch on skin.

I went to my mother's closet, and I opened the folding doors, and I touched the red dress. I was alone in the house. There was nobody to stop me, nobody to see. The barriers between my dream life and my waking one had been let down. My own clothes felt like a mistaken costume; quickly I took them off and threw them under the bed, where I wouldn't have to look at them. Now I was alone with the mass of dresses, the colors spilling out into the dim light, the disorderly crowd of shoes on the floor. Dresses and dresses, but there was only one for me. I was almost exactly my mother's size. My skin was soft as hers was, softer. I could feel the softness of my own skin. I slipped the dress on, the red dress. I looked at the lipsticks, the bottles of perfume; I looked at my shoulders in the mirror. A strange face stared back at me, a girl's face, mine.

A car door slammed shut outside.

I ran to the window—stupid boy, stupid boy—and that was where she saw me, maybe nothing more than a flash of red but she saw me. In a moment she would be in the house and upstairs and what would happen after that? I couldn't imagine. I took my clothes and ran to my room, closing the door behind me as the front door opened and closed downstairs but it was no use—there was no time. She was bound to find me. She had already found me. I sat at the edge of my bed and waited.

She didn't come.

A minute passed, another minute. As quietly as I could, I slipped out of the dress, into my boy's clothes, watched over by models and dinosaurs. I opened my door as gently as I could and put the dress back in the closet. When the door was closed, everything was where it had started. I went back to my room and waited, but she wasn't coming up. After ten or fifteen minutes, I went downstairs. She was waiting in the kitchen.

"How are you feeling, sweetie?" she asked, putting the cereal box in the pantry, the milk in the refrigerator door. She didn't even look.

"I'm fine," I told her.

"I'm glad to hear it," she said, and that was all. She looked at me once, and I knew that she had seen me, if ever I had doubted it. But we never spoke about it—never spoke about that afternoon, or Kendellan, never spoke openly to each other again. She was still my mother, I was still her son. But everything after that was in code, ambiguous, the silences full of unasked questions, the words empty of answers. And now I am grown, and my mother is dead, and my father is dead. And this is all the childhood I will ever have.

Sleepers Holding Hands

The telephone rang at half past midnight. You better come get him, said the stranger woman's voice—neighbor, busybody. I saw the lights on in the middle of the night and went over there and found him. He was sitting in the kitchen, eating peanut butter.

Dr. Parker's mind, cobwebbed with dreams, struggled to place itself: Here am I, and my daughter is—where? His wife,

Mary Ann, slept beside him, the rise and fall of her breath, like waves.

Has anybody seen his mother?

Nobody knows. Her car's still there.

Has this happened before?

But she doesn't answer. He can hear her shrug through the telephone: nothing, nevermind, none of her business. 12:34 in the morning, exactly.

You ought to come now, said the neighbor-lady.

In the morning?

I could call the protective service, they can come get him. They've been out here before.

No, Dr. Parker said. I don't want to trouble them.

He can't stay here.

Just wait till I get there, a couple of hours. Please. I'll start now.

All right, she said. Then hung up.

Dr. Parker slipped out of the sheets, his hairy knobby spidery legs shining white in the moonlight. Thought of waking his wife, but he didn't wish to be talked out of this. Which she would do. She would say: You're just making it possible for her to keep on living like this, to keep on behaving like a child. She couldn't do it without you. . . .

Years of practice—the telephone ringing when he was on call—had taught Mary Ann to sleep through anything. Dr. Parker opened the bedroom door with a burglar's noiseless touch. And why did a man of his sixty-two years wear a T-shirt to sleep in, like a college boy, instead of pajamas? Because she wants me to wear pajamas, he thought. Because we quarrel. My daughter is missing.

There were jeans in the laundry but he thought he might need authority. He dressed in plaid and chino, safe. Penny loafers, all from the same department store. He drove the Mercedes. He took his checkbook.

He had been retired for only a few months, but already this sky was strange to him, the dark and hush of the middle of the night. In the night it was cold September, though it would be summer again for a couple of hours at midday. He pulled over at a fishing access site, a few miles outside of town, went down to the river and pissed on the round rocks at the water's edge. Looking up into the spray of stars, the Milky Way thrown from some huge invisible hand, Dr. Parker wondered where his life had gone off the rails. It was in the marriage somewhere. LeeAnn was proof of it, a mother who could just up and leave her own son for no reason at all. Last time, she wasn't in jail or even in trouble—she met a musician in a traveling band and left with him for Portland, after knowing him eight hours. She called from Ritzville. At least she called last time.

When he got back in the Mercedes, Dr. Parker took a little sip from the bottle under the seat.

I'm all right, he said to himself, I'm all right.

A boy had come into his office at the clinic one day with a thyroid problem, a young man, really, one of these aging college students. Of course he didn't have insurance. And the thing was, he could have had money as easily as the next fellow—he was clearly intelligent and seemed to be from a good family. And he was older than Dr. Parker had been when Dr. Parker was first in practice. It was nothing as clear-cut as a dislike of the boy. But he didn't like the idea of saddling the clinic with the costs of the various CAT scans and PET scans and so on, just to save the boy a little discomfort, when he clearly had neither the means nor the intention to pay for them.

Instead he used the old technique, the one he had been taught many years before: extracting the material from the thyroid with a large, a very large needle, straight through the front of the neck.

This was still a perfectly safe technique, and in fact produced results that were more reliable than the gadgets. But he could still remember the boy's eyes widening at the sight of the needle. The boy complained, as Dr. Parker knew he would. And a few of his colleagues at the clinic, who had been scolded by Dr. Parker at one time or another, took this opportunity to get their small revenge. Really, it would have blown over in a few weeks. Nobody had been hurt.

Instead, Dr. Parker awoke one clear spring morning to discover that he had retired. He still wasn't quite sure how it had happened. One thing had led to another. Dr. Parker was no great appreciator of the modern world; homosexuals, for instance, still frightened and irritated him, and he was in no great hurry to welcome them into his world. And he felt that the thrill of mastery of new machines had taken the place of real medicine—that his colleagues in the clinic were turning into button-pushers and pill-dispensers instead of real doctors. But he had not intended to retire.

I'm all right, he said to himself, I'm all right. He took another little homeopathic sip of whiskey and followed his headlights, feeling the river running off to his left, the green force of the thing. Here he had spent the summer fishing—the fly rod still nestled in its case in the trunk, the twenty-pocketed vest filled with the most expensive of everything—and rather than think about LeeAnn any further, he decided to concentrate on the waters, and on the fish he had caught. In June he had been chased by a moose. In September, just a couple of weeks before, he had caught a twenty-eight-inch brown trout with spots on his sides the size of silver half-dollars.

It was four in the morning when he made Great Falls, still dark. He didn't know where his daughter's house was, only the address, which left him standing in the parking lot of a closed filling station, peering at the map in the middle of the phone book, trying to decode the tiny type. Idiots! Cheapskates! They could make it big enough to read. It wouldn't cost them anything.

It was almost five by the time he found LeeAnn's house. It lay inside the city but the streets were potholed dirt, hepatic yellow under the yellow streetlights. The fixtures were set on poles that seemed to be extraordinarily tall, so the light fell down dim but evenly, full of dust. The lawns were decorated with broken boats and tire swings. LeeAnn herself seemed to have an extra car in her driveway. The navy-blue Hyundai that Dr. Parker had bought her rested next to a yellow Pinto wagon with wood-grain sides.

He fought the familiar sag and panic. She would get through somehow. After every crisis there were a few good weeks, even months. At least Kendall—the one that Dr. Parker had liked so well, who had turned out to be a wife-beater—was safely behind bars in Arizona someplace.

You her father?

He recognized the voice—the woman on the telephone—but when he turned his head, she was somebody different! This woman was not old, as he had pictured her. She was not crabbed up or dirty. Instead she was a nice-looking blond woman with tight pants and a lot of black eyeliner.

Grandfather, Dr. Parker stumbled. The child, you know.

He's inside, sleeping.

The woman stepped back, looked at him and his Mercedes. It was like wearing your wallet on the outside of your pants.

No sign of LeeAnn? asked Dr. Parker.

Not a peep, the woman said. Look, you want to come inside for a while? The boy didn't get to sleep until a couple hours ago. He was crying for a while.

I don't want to put you out.

She laughed—and Dr. Parker understood that it was cigarettes that put the rasp in her voice, her raggedy laughter. A smoker.

I'd be at work, anyway, she said. I already took tonight off. You might as well come on in.

She turned in his headlights and walked off toward the little yellow house, and Dr. Parker noted her tight black pants and baby-blue sweater, noted that she was a little big for these things, and that she wobbled when she walked. Like a dream out of some other time, the way she was dressed—like a girl from *West Side Story*, or one of the Shirelles. He parked in the dirt in front of her house and remembered, all at once, that he had not slept and he had not eaten, that it was the middle of the night. It seemed to catch up to him as soon as he shut the engine off.

I'm all right, he told himself, I'm all right. He took another little sip of whiskey and followed her inside.

The house that he walked into—she left the door ajar—was so much bigger than the one he had seen from outside that he almost went outside again, to see if the little yellow house—a yellow that looked like it had come out of someone's body, somehow—could really hold the inside, which seemed to stretch away into darkness at the corners. The woman stood at a table, in a pool of light. Behind her, glass doors went out to a garden. A breeze was rubbing some of the leaves against the glass, making a scratchy sound.

You want anything to drink? the woman asked.

Bourbon, if you've got any. Bourbon on the rocks. I'm Peter Parker, by the way.

I know, she said. I called you, remember? Dr. Peter Parker.

She left him standing adrift in the middle of the big dark room: sofas around the edges, and big dim paintings behind them, things he couldn't quite make out. Plants. A coffee table sat in front of one of the sofas with several inoffensive magazines neatly piled on it, the headline of each peering out from under the others, like a waiting room in a bank, he thought, like a waiting room.

I don't like your daughter, Dr. Parker, and she doesn't like me.

No, he said, taking the cocktail glass.

I wasn't going to let the boy sit over there by himself all night, she said. Go ahead, sit down.

She aimed her own glass—not her first of the evening, Dr. Parker would wager a year's retirement on it—in the direction of one of the couches, and Dr. Parker sank down, sipping hot bourbon around the cold ice.

She perched on the arm of another sofa and lit an absurdly long white cigarette. That's bad for you, Dr. Parker thought.

How old is he, anyway? Seven or eight?

He's ten, said Dr. Parker. He's always been small for his age.

He was crying and crying, the woman said. Not when I found him there but after I brought him back here, after I called you. Said he just wanted to stay there and wait for her. What if she doesn't come? I asked him. Who's going to get you to school and all?

Where are you from? Dr. Parker asked.

Why?

You sound like you're from North Carolina, Dr. Parker said. I'm from North Carolina myself.

No kidding. What part?

Oh, he said, Durham, you know.

That's interesting, she said. How'd you end up out here?

Dr. Parker realized, when she asked this, that he did not wish to talk about his wife in front of this woman. He was all alone here, unmoored, adrift. On the other hand: He looked down at his wedding ring, engulfed in the flesh of his finger like a wire fence grown into an apple tree, and there was no point in lying.

When he looked up, she did, too, and he knew that she had been looking at his wedding ring when he had.

My wife had people out here, Dr. Parker said. My parents had passed by then, and we wanted to live near somebody. How about you?

A series of accidents, she said. Nothing too interesting.

Well, said Dr. Parker. And the silence seemed to rush up out of the corners of the room, engulfing him, though she seemed quite at home in it. It was very late. The clink and rattle of ice in his glass, the sparky sound her cigarette made as she drew smoke from it, all the small things seemed suddenly present. The woman—he still did not know her name—slid gently off the arm of the sofa and down into the seat, curling her legs beneath her, catlike.

I miss the summertime down there, she said. It's a strange thing!

It gets hot, said Dr. Parker.

Gets hot and stays hot, the woman said. Weeks on end. I never thought I'd miss it. Truth be told, I bet I wouldn't like it much if I did go back. But it's still the thing I think about.

I know.

Watching the sweat run down the outside of your glass of iced tea.

I know it, Dr. Parker said. The summer here is nice, though.

Too short, she said. Too short and not nearly hot enough. It isn't summer until you can sit outside at night with a summer dress on, you know.

You're right.

You can't do that in August here!

Well, you're right, he said. Not too many people would trade you, though. A lot of people like it here, in the summer, anyway.

It's true, she said.

You can feel the winter coming now, though, can't you?

Abruptly she sat up, out of her dream, like she had heard something. Car wheels crunched on the gravel outside.

One second, she said, stubbing her cigarette and moving indolently toward the door. Dr. Parker heard an engine shut off, a door slam, a man's voice saying something about how he was driving by and he saw the lights were on.

I'm busy right now, she told the man outside. I'm sorry.

The man said something Dr. Parker couldn't make out.

No, that's all right, she told him. Thanks for stopping by, though.

She closed the door and then stood for a moment with her back to the door, her hands behind her resting on the doorknob, as if she meant to keep an evil spirit from gaining entrance. Parker stood up himself. When she pulled the curtain back to watch the car drive away, Dr. Parker saw that it was a police car.

I guess I might as well be moving along, he said.

Let the boy sleep, the woman said.

This was an invitation. Now he saw it clearly.

Have another drink, the woman said. Can I get you another drink?

Now was the time to leave. Dr. Parker saw this clearly, too. Now was the time to wake the boy, pack the car with a few of his things, hit the road. He could clearly picture Mary Ann asleep in their marriage bed. He tried to summon the image of the boy sleeping, the rise and fall of his breath, the innocence of it, but it was no use.

I could use another drink, he said, carrying his empty glass over to the little table at the side of the room. He saw, with some small panic, that the big dim painting behind the drinks table was a nude, that all the paintings that lined the room were nudes.

She was waiting for him at the table. She was standing, waiting, level and calm. Dr. Parker was the one who was fluttering. She was there if he wanted her.

Dr. Parker set his drink down.

They were not teenagers. They were decorous, slow and careful, though the touch of her actual skin beneath her sweater, firm and yet soft, drove Dr. Parker crazy. It took them a minute before they kissed, faces looking past each other. Dr. Parker closed his eyes. And when they did kiss, it turned out Dr. Parker was much taller than this woman, whose name he still did not know, and so they had to approach the kiss carefully, slowly, to keep it from becoming comedy. Her mouth tasted of whiskey and cigarettes. Her tongue thrust into his mouth, deeper, searching, in a way that Mary Ann would never.

After a minute or two of this, not nearly long enough, she broke off and stood a little ways from him, staring into his face as if the answer to some definite question lay in it. Dr. Parker felt dizzy and drugged like he had been awakened from some deep dream. His hand—he couldn't help it—reached toward her again, up under the fuzzy blue of her sweater.

This seemed to decide her. She took his hand and led him into the bedroom, which was papered in red wallpaper and which had candles on the bedside table and mirrors on the ceiling. This woman is a whore! thought Dr. Parker. Not merely lonely and a little drunk. But this was nothing he wanted to think about. He put the thought aside and let himself be led to the edge of the bed, where the woman turned to him and touched him through the thin cloth of his chinos, as if she were making certain. Her touch was almost more than Dr. Parker could bear; he flinched from her hand, and then she was on her knees before him, untying his shoes, unzipping his pants, rolling his socks into careful little balls and placing them inside his shoes. This woman was in no hurry at all. When Dr. Parker was naked, she led him to the bed, let him recline there while she slowly removed her own clothes, article by article.

The door, he managed to say. It locks, doesn't it?

I already did.

I just . . . , he said. The boy . . .

Be quiet, she said.

Afterward, he could remember almost nothing definite but fragments: the way her skin felt in the heat of the little room, the curve of her hip in candlelight, sweat and perfume. She wore some common perfume, Dr. Parker never learned the name of it but he would run across it in all sorts of unexpected places, and the scent would bring him right back to this night, this room, this red wallpaper. There was no more talking. She knew what she was doing.

And then daylight was leaking around the edges of the heavy curtains, and Dr. Parker was dressing while she watched him from the bed. He felt an odd pride. Not that he was beautiful or even close, but he was good enough.

Thank you, Dr. Parker said.

My pleasure, said the woman.

When he left her there, though, and went out into the larger room, the boy was awake and watching out the window.

Timmy, said Dr. Parker.

Where were you?

Like touching a wire: This was daylight, his actual daylight life. These things had happened, and the boy had seen— what? What did the boy know? Dr. Parker searched his face in vain.

I was taking a nap, Dr. Parker said. The neighbor lady said you didn't get to sleep till late. I thought I would let you rest.

The boy turned his eyes from Dr. Parker's face, quickly. Impossible to read what he knew, or what he thought.

She still isn't come home yet, the boy said.

She didn't say anything to you?

This was the wrong question—the one the boy had been asking himself since she left. He looked up at Dr. Parker with his eyes filling quickly and the anger that he had been found out. Dr. Parker reached for the boy, but it was too late—the tears had already come, the boy had closed up on himself again. All Dr. Parker could do was hold him, the hard outer shell of him, and wait for him to subside.

As he waited, he heard the bedroom door click open, a few inches. She was watching them in a red satin bathrobe with Chinese birds embroidered on it. In the dawn light, her face looked hard and hollow. Everybody looked older.

Come on, Dr. Parker said to the boy. We'll go get you some clothes. You can come stay with us for a couple of days.

I don't want to.

Just for a couple of days, Dr. Parker said. Just till she comes back, or calls.

What if she's hurt someplace?

She's not, Dr. Parker said—because, in fact, she wasn't hurt someplace. LeeAnn was simply up to her old tricks again. She was driving across Nebraska with a carnie she had met someplace, or holed up in a Holiday Inn shooting heroin. She was drinking in the airport bar. She was learning to ride a motorcycle, or watching the sun rise over the Atomic Test Range in Nevada.

Let's go get your clothes, he said to the boy, and ushered him out the door before he could see the red satin bathrobe. Let some things remain a mystery.

One second, said the neighbor woman.

Dr. Parker looked back, and she was standing in her own doorway, just open a crack. There was nothing untoward.

Wait here, he told the boy, and left him standing in the dirt yard between the two houses.

I'm sorry, he said to the woman. It's time for me to go.

That's all right.

She waited, and he didn't know what she was waiting for. After a minute it came to him.

You had to miss work last night, he said. To take care of him, I mean. Could I make up for it?

No, that's all right, she said.

He reached his wallet out of the pocket of his chinos and peered into the folded money: fresh twenties, crisp from the automatic teller. I'm all right, he told himself. I'm a doctor. I have money.

Would a hundred do? he asked.

It would help out, she said. It's just the missing work and all.

It's no problem at all, he said, handing the money to her, feeling—the last thing—the touch of her soft hand as she took the money from him.

I'll see you again, he said to her.

You're welcome, said the woman. Anytime.

The door slipped shut behind him and there was the boy, out in the yard, staring.

That was nice of her to take you in, Dr. Parker told him.

I would have been fine.

Well, I hope so, Dr. Parker said. You can never tell.

I would have been fine, the boy said firmly.

LeeAnn's little house was unlocked. There was a shotgun in plain sight in the front hall closet, and Dr. Parker supposed it was loaded. Dirty dishes collected in the sink. It was like looking inside her mind, the mess of it. Dr. Parker tidied up while

Tim packed a duffel bag. He did the dishes and he wondered where he would end up this time. So far he had been to Baltimore once and Florida once and Nevada three times. Once he had even bought a ticket for Hawaii, but it turned out she was only in Tacoma, Washington. My child, he thought, my one and only child, my love. What would my life be without you? He found himself whistling, as he dried the dishes, as he waited for the boy.

Little Debbie

I know what she's dreaming about: chocolate cakes and strawberry pies, french fries and ice cream, whipped cream, custard cream, Devonshire cream and buttered toast. I know what turns her on. It makes me jealous sometimes.

I'm sitting in the ladder-back chair next to our bed and I'm, say, tipsy, and I'm watching her body rise and fall with her breathing. The light is coming through the open window from the yard light, yellow. I'm listening to the crickets. It's the end of summer, still too hot to have the house opened up, but Deb doesn't like to be cooped up in the A.C. She sleeps with just a sheet on under the big fan, nothing on but a pair of white panties that make her look even more tan than she is, and the sheet is twisted around and rumpled so it doesn't cover much. It's better than *Playboy*.

The trouble starts when she wakes up. She pulls the sheet up over her and says, What are you looking at?

I'm looking at you.

Don't, she says. Cut it out. I was *sleeping*.

Go back to sleep. I didn't mean to wake you.

You go on, she says—and then a minute later, when I'm still around, she says it again. Go on! I don't like it.

What?

When you look at me like that.

Like what?

She doesn't say anything, just stares at me with her arms folded tight against her ribs, holding that sheet against her, tight. There's nothing for me here. There's nothing for me in the living room, either, which is how I got here in the first place. But it's either that or go to bed and lie there in the dark next to her while she's sleeping and think about what it would be like to touch her with my hands, which ends up with me doing exactly that and Deb waking up pissed. Sleep is sacred business in our house. Sometimes I think her dream life, that other life of pies and ice cream, is more important than the one she lives with me. But this isn't an askable question. It isn't Englishable.

So I get a beer and then—because I'm sad, because my wife has just turned me out, because tomorrow is Sunday and besides I-don't-give-a-shit is descending, whatever, anything's enough—I fish the Jim Beam out of the back of the cupboard, ice cubes, pour myself a dose. I don't like to see you like that, Deb says. That's part of the reason she's in bed early on Saturday night. On the other hand, the fact that she's in bed early on a Saturday night and not up late with me, having fun or watching satellite TV is a big part of why I'm into the Jim Beam right now. It's a vicious circle.

She doesn't like to be looked at because she used to weigh over 300 pounds and I guess over 350 at one point in high school. The pictures from her first wedding are something. It's hard to tell what's the bride and what's the cake.

We don't have a lot of pictures around the house compared to most people. I mean, we've got her sister's kids on the refrigerator, but the big elaborate frames with the ski trips and family Christmases are out. It's like she didn't exist until four or five years ago, like a full-grown 120-pound baby born out of that 350-pounder. People turn their lives around, it's true. I tell people about what she used to weigh, and they just stare at her, just out-and-out stare, looking for evidence of the fat girl. I know why she doesn't like to be looked at.

There isn't any sign, though, not till you touch her. Then you can sometimes feel these little lines or ridges under the surface of her skin, from where it stretched out and then stretched back again, a crazy thing, like the birth of a child. I mean, how could a thing like that happen? The same exact skin that once held three of her. She had a couple of operations, one to get her boobs hitched up again—the ligament or whatever—and then I guess the underside of her chin. But you can't see the scars, you can't see anything, especially not when she's got a tan, which is always. I offered to buy her a tanning bed of her own for Christmas the other year, she's already got a StairMaster and a Schwinn exercise bike down in the basement. But she said no, she likes going in to the Tanfastic. She doesn't like being cooped up in the house all the time, she says. Which is what? I don't know.

I think about the touch of her skin and I get lonely for her. Turn on Channel 21, the skin channel, and I get even lonelier. What's worse than watching other people fucking? Not even fucking, just pretending. And then the bodies that the girls have, not even touched, not even used. That's one of my theories: People just want to see them get messed up a little, want to see them get used the way the rest of us have been used. I've got a lot of little theories. That's the thing about working with your hands, it gives you more time to think than it gives you things to think about. You realize after a while that the brain isn't always king. For instance I'm sitting here watching the skin channel because I'm lonely, and this is the one thing that makes me even more lonely. I could be watching a documentary on ancient Persia or a midget-sprint-car race. For another example, I get up and get another dose of Jim Beam. This particular decision goes like this: I'm fucked anyway so I might as well.

It isn't even two yet.

I don't know how great we're doing.

Debbie didn't lose all that weight just to find me. She lives on fizzy water and carrot sticks and boneless skinless chickens, she suffers. I'd be disappointed if she didn't have hopes and dreams beyond this: a horse, I know she wants a horse, and some new stuff for the living room that doesn't come from Sears this time. That isn't even the start of it though. There's something driving her. I see her down on the StairMaster, climbing up to nowhere with a towel around her neck to catch the sweat, and she's got this look on her face. She's not even seeing me. I used to think this was funny, there's a place next to the Winn-Dixie that's got about fifteen of the stair machines in the window next to each other, and you'd see the secretaries and the girls from the community college walking up the ladder to nowhere. We made jokes about wiring those suckers up to run the lights. With Debbie, though, that stairway is going somewhere. She's only twenty-eight. I get another drink to celebrate her success.

I move a porch chair out into the middle of the lawn and light a cigar. I'm having all kinds of good ideas.

The chair is the springy-metal kind with the shell back, and it makes a noise when I run into the porch rail, and again when I move it out of the harmful radiation of the yard light and into the shadow of the house. That yellow light cannot be good for you. In the dark, though, I can't see the twirls and curves of the cigar smoke, only the red bumblebee of the coal. They say that blind people don't smoke because they don't get the pleasure of seeing it. And out beyond that circle of light is the whole country. One little slip and you could end up in Grand

Rapids, Tampa, anywhere—you could just come loose, dislocated. I could, anyway. I didn't grow up here. I've got an ex-wife and a daughter named Tiffany, a day's drive away from here. Tell me how I ended up going along with the name Tiffany and you'll have the key. Along with many other things, it's a mystery to me. Like this: Debbie's face when we end up in the girls' section of Penney's or Sears, looking for a birthday treat for my daughter, she gets a hungry look on her face when she walks among all that pink and lace. There's no other word for it: a *hunger*. She *wants* these things. A big pink cake, waiting for her, I see her fingers when she was fat, sneaking frosting when she thought nobody was looking. The hands of really fat people, there's something about them: the way big drooping arms end up in tiny hands.

Somewhere in here I decide that I might justaswell bring the fifth of Jim Beam out onto the lawn with me and I light another cigar besides. What? It's like running a car into a bridge abutment and surviving. Sunday morning is never coming. Debbie's going somewhere. She didn't lose 225 pounds just to find me, I know that much, anyway, and the certainty makes me tremble and sweat. All those highways, FM country the same in every town, a McDonald's on every highway corner, it makes me want to throw up. My great-grandfathers would be ashamed of me, and rightly so. You know what pisses me off? Everything pisses me off. What? Every time she passes the refrigerator, she's not eating something. I just think of what's going on in her imagination, in her dreams of T-bone steaks with a half-inch ring of fat, hot off the barbecue, bread and butter and more butter on the corn, MoonPies and RC Cola, chopped-pork BBQ on a bun, bear claws and cream horns, pepperoni pizza, all you can eat. I take a drink straight out of the whiskey bottle and I see that I am *living the dream*. The words make me laugh but it's the truth: all the whiskey I can stand to drink, just keep going, follow the thing through: greedy, grasping, like Debbie lost in a supermarket bakery after hours, the pink icing all to herself, living the dream, down on her knees behind the cooler cases of pies and cookies, buttercream braids, French twists, raspberry-swirl cheesecake, I take a drink of Jim Beam straight out of the bottle and I'm laughing hard enough to spill a little down onto my shirt but it's no big deal, I'm living the dream, there's plenty left to kill me.

Jim, she says, come to bed. It's time for you to come to bed.

She's out on the lawn in her T-shirt and panties. I could explain to her—living the dream, how we're the same—but then I see that this is not the case. I have been doing something dirty, and she has caught me at it.

Sorry, I tell her. The word comes out of my mouth blurry.

You fucker, she says. Put the cigar out and come to bed.

I have been forgiven, I can tell by the way she talks.

I ask her, Come here for a second.

It's *bedtime*, Jim. It was bedtime a long time ago.

Come here for a second.

I can't see her face in the dark but I know that dirty look. I have sinned, and I have been forgiven, and I am suddenly light. She comes over and sits down in my lap (this is extra, more than I could hope for), and she doesn't weigh anything, this is the flying dream where we don't have any gravity anymore and everything is possible. We look up into the stars and they are spinning in front of our eyes, drunk. Our little story goes forward one more day.

Scarecrow

Texas, day three: scablands stretching either side of the high-way, greasewood, horses, trailers, dusty-looking mountains on the far curve of the earth. Dan is driving, a steady fifty-five.

Any faster and the U-Haul trailer chained to the back bumper will start to shimmy and buck. Any slower and they wouldn't be moving at all. The big Crown Victoria (her father gave it to them) lunges over the buckled blacktop like a slow boat, toward the distant mirages, which appear and disappear. They don't exactly look like water.

Rhonda is either asleep or awake, her face against the hot glass, a half-finished crossword puzzle on the seat between them. She works in ink. Experimentally—this speed does not demand his attention—Dan reaches over to touch her bare thigh, his hand under the hem of her big shorts.

She slaps his hand away without opening her eyes. What time is it? she asks.

Quarter to eleven, he says.

It's hot, she says, can you turn on the A.C.?

It is on, Dan says.

Can you put it on more?

He slides the lever another half inch colder, doing her a favor, with a faint exasperated look that she doesn't open her eyes to see. The argument they are not quite having rests in the air between them, along with the faint beginnings of a light-struck headache. One too many cigarettes, he thinks, last night in the motel. He remembers little empty airline bottles of gin, lined up like soldiers on the television set.

Then nothing for a few miles longer.

They're moving to the desert, to Tucson.

Dan is looking at the curvature of the earth, the line of the horizon, which in this place is not a line at all but a blurring, dust and aerial perspective bleeding the blue sky into the gray dirt. Even the plants are gray, with black stems. He doesn't know what to call them: bushes? weeds? Spiky and poisonous, they look like nothing in North Carolina, where he and Rhonda are both from. A scarred look, like burn survivors. Somewhere in the last twenty minutes, they passed into another country and now there are no more horses, no more trailers, only fences, survivor-plants and sky.

Then he sees it: black bundle of rags by the side of the highway. A man.

He touches the brakes and the trailer-coupling bangs, the rear end dips, her eyes now open and on him.

What is it? Rhonda asks.

He can't see around the orange pig trailer. He can't tell if he saw anything or not.

A person, Dan says. I think.

Where?

The side of the road. He was just lying there, Dan says. You think we ought to go back?

Rhonda says, I didn't see him. I don't know.

The road unwinds in front of them, a mile, three miles. He doesn't turn, he doesn't stop. An afterimage printed on his retina, the black thing in the sun.

You're going to stop, aren't you? Rhonda asks.

I don't even know what it was, he says. A bag of trash. It could have been anything.

It's a hundred and five, she says.

You want to go back?

I don't think *want to* is the right way to say it, Rhonda says. I think we have to. I hope somebody would do it for me.

All right, he says after half a mile of thought. All right.

But if she had not been in the car with him, had not been

watching, he would have kept on driving. Somehow they both know this. He finds a spot, he turns back, all the time with her eyes on him. Fear, good sense, or cowardice. Words. Something has just happened.

The black bundle is still there.

He still can't tell what it is, going the wrong way, going too fast. Rhonda freezes when she sees it, turns when they pass it, but the pig of a trailer is in the way. She rolls her window down and the hot air floods in like the door of an oven. She reaches over and turns the A.C. off. I couldn't see, she says.

I know.

I couldn't tell; maybe it was nothing. Maybe you were right.

No, he says. You were right. We have to find out. We're going in the wrong direction anyway.

She puts her hand on the bare skin of his arm. He can shut up now. She means it kindly but Daniel does not wish to be forgiven for a thing he hasn't done, or hasn't left undone. They've only been married a year, they haven't made all their compromises yet. Despite living in sin three years before wedding, this still feels like a new start, a brand-new life. He still hears quotation marks around the words: "Husband." "Wife."

We don't have to, Rhonda says.

For Christ's sake, Daniel says. One way or the other. You can't have it both ways.

The anger comes easily in the hot wind pouring through the windows. If only he had let his concentration slip across the center line, or into the distance, anywhere but the roadside bundle. None of this needed to happen. It seems like Rhonda's fault but it is not her fault; except that he was relying on her fear for his own escape. We don't have to, dear. Somebody will take care of him. It's somebody's job.

How do you suppose he got there? Rhonda asks. It's like he dropped from the sky.

He knows, all at once, they do not belong here. They will not. Here, under the dust-colored sky, where everything is spiked or fanged or poisonous, where at noon the ground is in the 130s, even in in the shade. They are children imitating grown-ups. They are playing in traffic. Daniel knows this, Rhonda doesn't, but he can't summon himself to say it: They have been playing at life. But this is real, this is final. This is beyond them.

Daniel finds a turnout and heaves the circus train—car, hitch, trailer—around. Two miles back and there he is.

A man, undoubtedly a man. Asleep or dead, by the side of the road.

Daniel eases the big car close and closer and then stops. Neither of them speaks. Neither makes a move to get out of the car. They watch him, looking for signs of breath. A message, to tell them what to do. This is utterly beyond them. Daniel looks at Rhonda. She looks at Daniel. They return their eyes to the man in black. He wears a suit coat and black shirt, black jeans, boots that have burst at the sides. His toes peek through the gap, brown and wrinkled like Greek olives. His face is hidden under the brim of a baseball cap. He doesn't move.

Rhonda says, Let's call somebody.

But the screen of the cell phone says OUT OF SERVICE

when she tries it, the square reassuring letters let them down. They are out of range, beyond help. They sit a minute longer, gathering themselves, each waiting for the other to move. What can they do for him? this scarecrow, desiccating by the side of the road, the flattened beer cans and the glitter of glass, hot wind sifting through the iron-gray branches. Discarded, Daniel thinks. Dead. But he must do something, anything. Rhonda expects it of him. Remember, he tells himself: when a man and a woman are at this end of things, it is always the man's turn. The rest is window dressing. New man and new woman. Sex roles for the nineties. He opens the door of the Crown Vic, gets out, walks over to the body.

The smell is concentrated: piss and alcohol. He doesn't seem to be breathing. A helplessness comes over Daniel, in the eyes of his wife. He wonders: What am I supposed to do? The Heimlich maneuver, he thinks, the old mouth-to-mouth—looking meanwhile at the black lips pulled back over yellow teeth, imagining the Kiss of Life. Flies and wind. His hands flap limp at his sides.

Hello? he asks, uneasy. Hello?

Not even knowing what the Spanish is.

Not a flutter. He looks back at the windshield, blind in the sun, where he knows his wife is watching. Daniel is failing, he can feel it. Some magic action he should know and doesn't, the technique of bringing the dead back to life. Spinning straw into gold. This was not the way it was supposed to be between them. New man and new woman.

But words don't matter here. Bleached bone in the sun. The windshield stares, the sun pales everything in its light.

Before he needs to touch him, though, before he can summon himself to action, a tan Texas Highway Patrol car drives onto the shoulder, scattering gravel, and lurches to a halt and a fat crew-cut man of Daniel's age gets out and prods the body with the toe of his boot.

Get up there, chief! the cop says. Come on, amigo. Time to get a move on. Get yourself a sunburn, lying there.

The body curls and uncurls, an inchworm movement on the ground. The cop prods again with his boot. The eyes crack slowly and then open. The sleeping man sits up, looks around like this is strange to him. Then gets to his feet and walks away.

The cop turns to Daniel: Can I ask what you were doing?

But he can't answer yet, he's watching the miracle, the resurrected body walking, gangling, off into the flat and featureless desert, growing smaller and smaller, walking toward the far gray hills and nothing in-between.

What they do, the cop says, one of them lies out like that, and another half a dozen will be out in the ditch. You wouldn't think they could hide in that. Then somebody comes along, somebody like you. The next thing you know, the car's in Nogales. We don't find the bodies.

Hot wind slipping through the branches. Black scarecrow, walking.

All I'm trying to say is y'all watch out for yourselves, the cop tells Daniel.

Gets back into his car and pulls away, leaves them blinking

in the hard light. It's still morning. They are learning to be strangers here. This is not home. This is not going to be. Daniel looks to the windshield, the door half open and his wife half out, looking at him like a stranger. She's finding something new about him, a new little something every day. Daniel's eyes strain toward the horizon, but the scarecrow is gone.

Little Palaces

Evelyn stands by the side of the highway, a hot breezy spring day, gluing ribbons and roses onto her cross. The cars hurtle by a few feet from her, a blast of wind and gravel that startles her, each one. Some of them, for some reason, honk. Fuck you, she thinks toward each of them, especially the honkers. Fuck you and you and you and you.

The bag from the Ben Franklin lies open at her feet, full of notions, knickknacks. She brought more plastic flowers than she thought she would need, which turns out to be good—the cross is much bigger than it looks to be from the roadway, an easy eighteen inches tall, white vinyl. The American Legion put it up to mark the spot where her parents died in October, seven months ago, vaulting over the borrow pit and into a tree in their new Westfalia camper, trying not to hit a deer, which they hit anyway. The trooper had offered her the deer meat. This was one of the things she always mentioned when she tried to explain to her friends back in college—*the fucking cop offered me the deer meat*—but it's like she's speaking Chinese or something. They just hear it as weird, they don't understand that it might be happening to somebody. Evelyn can feel herself fading from their lives, a little smell, slowly dissipating.

Yet another thing I find strange, she thinks to herself, imagining what it would be like to talk to somebody. Yet another thing she finds strange is that a few days ago, people began decorating their crosses—or somebody's crosses, anyway, she isn't sure what the rules of ownership are. Evelyn is a stranger here. Her parents had just retired to this cloudy, foggy, cold valley—retired young, as her father was in shaky health—and built a nonrustic prefabricated log cabin. Before her mother could get the towels and curtains hung, they were dead. Back from California to tend to the details, Evelyn missed too many classes to finish the semester, and then there was the cabin to sell, and then there's the whole idea that she now has all her parents' money and insurance and so on and she (the only child) will be worth, once the real estate clears, about nine hundred thousand dollars.

So: Rich Evelyn spent the winter poking through her parents' stuff and going stir-crazy while the snow piled up outside, living on frozen lasagna and satellite TV, building huge fires in the stone fireplace. *I have my mother's eyes*, she thought to herself, *and my father's oxygen tank.* By spring she felt like the subject of some awful experiment. She emerged into the daylight, blinking, riding her mother's pink bicycle between the crusty patches of snow and the defrosting deer carcasses. It was unbelievable how many deer died along this road—the only north-to-south road through the valley, a tunnel of ice and shade all winter. The natives, Evelyn noticed, drove enormous pickup trucks, high off the ground, with elaborate grille guards made out of pipes and stout metal. No avoidance for them. A deer in those headlights better figure out how to move.

Also killed were people. The white crosses were piled up on every curve, three and four and five to a pole. From her bike—a scary ride anyway, with trucks the size of locomotives whizzing by, inches away from her butt—Evelyn wondered how this one sparsely populated valley could keep up the carnage. Wouldn't they run out of people? Or maybe, she thought, maybe it was just summer visitors and fresh retirees that they harvested. Some secret back way that the locals took. They would never tell Evelyn, with the ruby in her nose and her black-and-pink hair.

She can feel them, driving by, looking at this strange creature, this *bicyclist*, and it makes Evelyn happy to think of what she looks like to them. There's another set of cross-decorators at the next curve, a hundred yards up, and every once in a while she can feel them looking at her. One of them is in a wheelchair. *I'm a weirdo, I'm a freak,* she thinks. *I'm not a basically happy person.* Last night she found a Dutch punk video on the satellite someplace and it made her happy, to think there were still people she might like, people who might like her, somewhere out in the world, even if none of them happened to be within a hundred miles of here.

For Mom, she thinks, gluing a big red heart with gold lace trim onto the base of the cross. *Sacred fucking bleeding heart,* Evelyn thinks, but somewhere in her is a real feeling, beyond the usual self-pity. All winter orphaned Evelyn has been stuck in herself—but now it's spring, and her mother will not see it. Her father will not drag his tank down to the river to fish. They will not suddenly appear in the bedroom to bust her for reading their letters, trying on their clothes. They're dead, they're gone, and in the sunshine and the budding trees this seems unbelievably sad.

"You want a beer?"

It's a girl in a van, and a man is driving, and then she sees that he's sitting in a wheelchair, and then she figures out that it's the two from up the road, the ones who were decorating their own cross. They seem friendly, though.

"I'm almost done," Evelyn says, like this is an answer. Dummy!

"We saw you working down here," the girl says. "It's a hot day for it."

A girl? When Evelyn looks more closely, it's hard to tell— she's wearing wraparound mirrored shades, like the ones bicyclists used to wear, which Evelyn has noticed are the latest redneck fashion craze. Tank tops and blue tattoos and bikie shades. This girl or woman is missing the tattoo, but she's got the tank top and the hair, Rod Stewart circa 1978, blond and roostery. She seems friendly enough, though, and Evelyn—she suddenly discovers—really needs to talk to somebody.

"I don't mind the heat," she says. "Not after this spring. It seemed like it rained every day!"

"It'll do that," says the woman in the van. "Just wait till June."

"It gets bad?"

"You'll think you lost your mind," the woman says. "Seriously, we've got a half case iced down in the back, and that is hot work you're doing on a day like today."

"Sure," says Evelyn on impulse, though she doesn't usually drink beer, and not at all lately, not since her butt exploded from sitting around on the couch all winter.

"Pull over," the woman says to the driver, back in the shadowy inside of the van, and he pulls it—leaning, listing—off the side of the road, and shuts the motor off. The quiet rushes in, the sound of the wind, which sounds sinister to Evelyn. What if they aren't OK? There's nobody to protect her, nobody in the world. Then the sliding side door turtles open and the woman is inside, handing Evelyn a cold, wet Pabst Blue Ribbon. One for the driver and one for herself. She rolls her shades up onto the top of her head, and Evelyn sees—in the crow's feet around her eyes, the sunburnt liver-marked backs of her hands and puckery knuckles and elbows—that she is at least thirty, maybe older. She only dresses like a kid.

"That was your parents?" the woman asks. "Last fall?"

Evelyn nods.

"Sorry to hear it," the woman says, steps all the way out of the van and offers her hand to Evelyn. "I'm Sherry Lewis," she says.

"And that's Lamb Chop driving, there?"

"What? How did you hear about that?"

"I keep telling you," says the guy in the wheelchair. "Everybody in the whole fucking world saw that show when they were growing up. Everybody but you."

"It's true," says Evelyn. "I think her show is still on."

"No, she died last year," the wheelchair guy says.

"That's Vic," says Sherry Lewis, pointing toward the dark cave of the van.

Evelyn steps up, a little nervously, peers in, and tries to make out Vic's face: a pointy triangle, raggedy hair like Peter Pan. He seems to be secretly amused, holding his beer between his hands, both of them stuck together into fists.

"I'm Evelyn," she says.

"Did you see Shari Lewis the last couple of years?" he says. "Man, if she'd ever had a good laugh or an orgasm, her face would have just fallen on the floor. She looked good, don't get me wrong, just a little too tight."

"She was scary, even before," Evelyn says.

"I couldn't agree more," Vic says, setting his beer can down on the cooler, offering her his folded hand to shake. Evelyn, awkward, eventually takes it between her own hands, a little lump of tendon and bone, skin chilly and wet from the beer. *We find ourself in Paradise*, she thinks.

"We're going to the lake," says Sherry Lewis. "You want to go to the lake with us?"

"Sure," Evelyn says, and as soon as she says it, the voices come thundering through her head: Danger! Danger! Danger!

"Actually, um," she says, "I'm on my bike."

"There's room in the back," Vic says.

"I don't even have my suit with me or anything!" Evelyn says brightly.

"We're not going *swimming*," Sherry Lewis says. "We're going *fishing*."

"She's not worried about that," Vic says. "She's worried they're going to find her disembodied torso in the woods someplace. Don't you read the *Weekly World News*?"

"Brother to brother: I want my kidney back," Evelyn says, her favorite headline of all last year.

"Doctors struggle to save baby found in fried chicken box," Vic says, and that settles it: They're friends.

"Give me a sec," says Evelyn, taking her beer down to the cross, which is basically finished. She can come back tomorrow, assuming she's still alive. Murder, drowning, car accident, and now here she is abandoning her own mother to go off with these two apparently fun but dangerous people. *I'm nineteen,* Evelyn thinks, sending the thought toward her mother. *I get to do this.*

"All set," she says, heaving the fat pink bike and the Ben Franklin bag into the back of the van. Vic is already strapped in behind the wheel, Sherry next to him, feet up on the dash.

"Just slide it, honey," Sherry says, pointing her head toward the door. "You can sit on the cooler."

It's like being in a cave, the back of the van, with the only light coming through the windshield. A little patch of sky. She watches with real fascination how Vic works the brakes and gas pedal with his hands, steering with his clumsy fists. This happened to him somehow, she thinks. How?

"You go to school?" Sherry asks her.

"Not right now," Evelyn says. "I've been up here taking care of the loose ends."

"It's amazing," Sherry says, "the amount of shit when somebody dies. You think it's going to be like the movies, where it's just boom, bang, all over. Three weeks later, you're still signing papers and meeting lawyers."

This woman is dumb as a dog, thinks Evelyn—not exactly what she wants to be thinking, but there it is.

"Who was that?" Evelyn asks. "Back there, I mean."

"My sister," Sherry Lewis says. "His girlfriend."

"I was there, too," says Vic.

"In a manner of speaking," Sherry says. She cranes her neck to look at Evelyn. "He passed out drunk behind the wheel. That's what happened. If he wasn't in that chair, he'd be in prison today."

"See?" Vic says. "Silver lining."

This seems to be some sort of a test. Were they actually fighting? The whole atmosphere of the two of them got suddenly harder to figure out: whether they were a couple or not, whether they even liked each other.

"How long ago?" she asks.

"Two years last Christmas," Sherry says.

"I'm really sorry," Evelyn says.

"Yeah, well," Sherry says. "Sorry and sorry and sorry. To tell you the truth, I'd like to be done with it, you know? I mean she was my sister, and I loved her and all. But Jesus Christ, I'm sick of it."

Evelyn looks at her, amazed. She didn't know you could say this secret out loud without being struck by lightning; she couldn't even feel it without being evil. Nobody's watching, it occurs to her. Nobody's keeping score. Mom and Dad are dead.

"It isn't going to rain, is it?" Vic says.

"How the hell would I know?" Sherry says, lighting a very long cigarette, watching the smoke slipstream out the open window.

The trees and sky blur by outside, a dreamy drifting sensation of speed. Then some random bumps and rattles, gravel on the wheel wells, and she knows they are on gravel, and then—a few bumps later—they are at the lake: a cloudy gray circle of water, closed in by tall, gloomy-looking pine trees, with a waterfall at the far end, surrounded by mountains that end in clouds.

"What happened to summer?" Evelyn asks. "It was nice a minute ago."

"Just you wait," says Sherry Lewis.

"You have been living here too long," Vic says. "It's making you sincere and depressing. You need to get out."

"What's wrong with sincere?"

Vic adjusts his chair squarely on the fold-down metal lift before he answers.

"I am never more ridiculous than when I am sincere," he says. "You might be different."

He lowers himself with a distant hydraulic whine. Evelyn notices the van is parked in the one KEEP OUT, $500 FINE handicapped parking spot, but there is nobody else in the parking lot, nobody else at the lake. All this protection for something that doesn't need protecting.

"Here we are in paradise," Vic says. "Where's my Pepe Lopez?"

"No fucking way, Vic," Sherry says.

"Let's have a fight."

"I'm not going to argue with you. But I'm damnsure not going to drive down that hill with you drunk again."

"You can drive, then."

"Those fucking hand controls," Sherry says, and turns to Evelyn as a referee. "Last time I tried to drive that damn thing, I took out two chickens and a mailbox."

"She has a Ph.D. in American Studies," Vic says. "You believe me?"

Evelyn looks from one to the other.

"Maybe I'll just take my bike and go," she says. "I don't want to spoil your fight."

"I'm not fighting," Sherry says. "Not yet. You won't have a hard time figuring it out."

"What?"

"When we start," Sherry says, unpacking the back of the van: cooler, tackle box, a tube-and-plastic recliner straight out of Kmart.

"Vic," says Sherry, drawing out the word into a long, whiny vowel. "Viiiiic. We forgot the fucking worms, Vic."

"No, they're in the cooler."

"They're not in the cooler, Vic."

"Look down at the bottom," he says, "one of those little styrofoam deals, you know, like potato salad comes in."

"Oh, fuck," Sherry says, "oh, ick," pulling one wet, icy worm from the cooler; and it occurs to Evelyn, here, that the top of her beer can tastes like *worm*.

Vic says, "Got loose in there, did they?"

"I feel like I am sliding into chaos, Vic," says Sherry Lewis. "I feel like my life is sliding into chaos and you are behind me, pushing."

"Did you come out here to talk or did you come to fish?" Vic says.

"I know that joke," says Evelyn.

But Sherry Lewis is weeping, of all things. Just when Evelyn was starting to enjoy herself: real tears, the way the face dissolves and shatters, crazy eyes and then she turns and she walks off by herself, a little trail that winds away from the parking lot, along the windswept shore. Whitecaps on the lake.

"Hey," Vic says, "wait."

"You fuck off," Sherry says over her shoulder. "Get the girl to bait your fucking worm."

And then she's gone, wind in the trees, Evelyn and Vic alone in the parking lot. She watches his face: a blank thing like a rock, watching Sherry go. He's a grown-up, Evelyn thinks, a hard set to his face. He has had experiences, learned to show nothing. Then he appears to realize, all of a sudden, that Eve-lyn is still with him.

"This has not been a good day for her," Vic explains.

"Not for you, either," Evelyn says. "I imagine."

"Every day is a sunshine day for me," he says. "Ever since I developed a positive mental attitude."

He laughs, and Evelyn laughs with him, uncomfortable as she can be. Nothing funny about the wheelchair, the hands compressed into tight bunches of fingers. Maybe he is talking about something else.

"Now I would like to fish," Vic says, like a king. "If you would be so kind."

"What do I do?"

"You put the rod in there," he says, nodding toward his right hand, "then you tie on one of those lure dudes. Open a beer and light a cigarette. There isn't anything to it."

Oh boy oh boy oh boy, she thinks: touch the hand. Pry the fingers loose. Not exactly anything she had in mind. But he is asking, and she is not going to say no to him, she is not going to fail this test. She follows him down to the dock—rickety wheels across the rough boards—and stands at the end, next to him, and together they watch the clouds move slowly across the deep green sides of the mountains.

"I want my summer back," says Evelyn.

"This *is* summer," Vic says. "This is what it looks like here. Give me a hand?"

She pries the fingers apart (soft spring of tendon under

the skin, not the callused claw she was expecting) then ties the big Rapala to the end of the monofilament, three inches of silver and sparkle and treble hooks. There's nothing gross, when she's actually doing it—just skin on skin, one hand touching another.

"Where'd you learn that?" Vic asks.

"What?"

"That knot, whatever it's called. The one where you tie on the hook."

"That's called a clinch knot," Evelyn says. "My father taught it to me. He used to take me fishing, sometimes, which I hated."

"Oh, good," Vic says, hauling the rod back, launching the lure with a complicated two-handed cast. The line sings out, and then—far out in the lake—the Rapala slips into the water with a small polite splash. Vic turns the handle to tighten the line, then waits for the sink.

"It's a little-known fact," Vic says, "that if you only felt a little bit worse about this whole thing, you could bring your father back to life! Both your parents. Isn't that amazing?"

"Incredible," Evelyn says.

"I felt so shitty last year that Lynn just rose straight up out of her grave."

"What's she doing now?"

"Waiting tables in Pittsburgh, I believe," Vic says. "We sort of lost touch. I think she's pissed at me."

"I could certainly understand why."

"Oh, it makes perfect sense. Not that I can do much about

it. It's all water under the bridge now, as my grandmother used to say."

Vic turns to her and grins—his hard, impervious smile.

"Sometimes I think I might go join her there," he says. "In Pittsburgh."

~   ~   ~

Three small brook trout and five cans of beer later—five cans of beer *apiece*—Sherry Lewis appears again.

"Doing any good?" she says, coming out of the brush by the dock.

"Nothing spectacular," Vic says.

"It's no kind of day for fishing," Sherry says. "Too cold." She hoists herself up the side rails of the dock and heaves herself over, surprisingly limber and quick. She is surprised to find Evelyn still there, apparently.

"I'm sorry I got mad with you," she says to Vic. "It's my period or something."

"It's all right. We're having fun."

We're having fun, Evelyn thinks. Me and Vic. Not you. But she feels herself disappearing as Sherry opens the cooler lid, rattles through the ice in search of a Pabst despite the three silver corpses of the fish.

"Little guys," Sherry says to Vic. "Good for eating, though."

Talking straight at him, like it's just the two of them, and Evelyn feels a momentary sense of panic. *I seem to be disappearing*, she thinks, holding her hand up to the sky to see if she can see through herself.

"You want to come over for dinner?" she asks them.

They look. Evelyn shrugs.

"I've got a gas grill," she says.

"I don't know," says Vic.

"We can stop at the IGA," says Evelyn. "I've got money. We can get anything we want. Marshmallows, Popsicles, the works. We can have a regular party."

"Not tonight," says Sherry Lewis. On cue, a cold wind blows over them from the lake and the three of them remember their dead; which is how we started out, Evelyn remembers. Vic (she watches his face) shuts up like a clam.

"We can get some alcohol, anyway," Evelyn says.

"Motherfucker!" Vic says, jumping—and it takes her a moment to figure out that he's got a fish on the line, a big fish this time. The line sings off the reel and the rod tip bends toward the lake.

"That's a nice fish," Sherry says.

But Vic ignores her, straining to keep the pressure on, tightening down the drag on the little Zebco reel. He reels a little line in but the fish takes it right back, right back and more, dancing and diving and tail-slapping all the way out of the water, and it is *exactly* like a fish her father caught—the same lake, the same line, the same fish—and Evelyn feels him there beside her, cursing under his breath, and he smelled of cigarette smoke and he had dirt under his fingernails and *he is still dead* and going to stay that way. . . .

And then the rod slips out of Vic's clumsy fingers and the rod is gone and the line is gone and so is the fish. Everything is quiet.

"Fuck me," Vic says.

"That was my fucking rod," Sherry says.

~   ~   ~

Vic and Sherry never quite decide where they want to go. More driving, Evelyn in the back again, with no idea where she is and no idea where she's going and nobody else knows, either. They stop at the state liquor store, buy a bottle of tequila and one of Jack Daniel's. Sherry buys with Evelyn's money.

Evelyn waits outside, too young to go in. In the parking lot, the sun is hot, the woods are alive with the drip and scurry of melting snow, runoff. The world is coming alive again. Taking off the winter coat. She feels the sap rising in her own veins.

"I can't believe you lost my fucking rod," Sherry says. Her face is flickery in the windshield light, wind ruffling the sun in the trees, she's looking at Vic and then at Evelyn, Vic then Evelyn. "That was my good rod," she says.

In the flickering light, her face looks to soften and fill, and Evelyn thinks: she's not so different from me. She's lost her sister. *Lost:* as if the sister, Evelyn's parents, Vic's legs were all mislaid someplace, some lonely bus station in Kansas or South Dakota with the dust and sunlight blowing through.

"I don't know," Vic says.

"What?"

"We can go over to her house," he says, causing Evelyn to disappear again. "We can cook the fish up over there."

"Is that what you want?"

Vic hunches his shoulders: OK.

"OK," says Sherry Lewis. "Whatever you want, Vic. I just want to stop off at the palaces and get my shit, just in case."

In case of what? thinks Evelyn. What kind of shit?

"Be a sweetie," Sherry says. "Toss me a coldie, won't you?"

Evelyn reaches, wrestles, bouncing against the metal sides of the truck, and then—as soon as she has accomplished the beer—the van stops, and the door slides open. Sherry takes the cold and dripping beer from her as she emerges, blinking, into the sun, socketing the can into a foam can cooler that reads: I AM THE SHIT THAT HAPPENS.

"I'm just going to run in," Sherry says. "Don't bother."

"Hold up," Vic says. "I need a little fixing."

"I'll be inside."

The palaces are single rooms, all in a horseshoe around a disused pond or fountain—a motel, once, but not for quite a while.

"You live here?" Evelyn asks Vic.

"I vegetate," he says, maneuvering the chair onto the metal-mesh lowering tray. A whir and whine of little motors. "I ruminate and urinate. Right back."

He wheels himself into the nearest shack, the one with the ramp, next door to Sherry Lewis's shack, and Evelyn looks around. The pool is rotten concrete, thirties concrete, cracked and broken, with moss growing in the cracks. HEIDELBERG HAUS says the sign out by the highway, and the whole complex looks out over the ass end of a restaurant: Dumpsters full of stale grease, tablecloths on a clothesline.

And what kind of "fixing" does a man in a wheelchair need? Where does Vic stop? Evelyn thinks of Conor, her off-again boyfriend back in California, a soft, floppy-haired boy who lived to play Frisbee golf, which he called "Folf," and also something called "Ultimate"—thinks about how soft he was, and how much harder Vic is. Evelyn knows she's comparing them, knows she's thinking about Vic as somebody to sleep with, if he can. She lets herself imagine: remembering Conor's fervent, selfish ineptitude. Not that Evelyn is an expert herself, exactly. What? Those hands, little balls of flesh.

She edges closer to the window, trying to hear what they are saying to each other inside. A silence: then the sound of a beer can kicked across a concrete floor, footsteps, slamming. Evelyn backs away quickly. Who? What? Not me.

"No, *you* fuck you," says Sherry Lewis, backing out of Vic's doorway into the sun, screaming into the black rectangle.

Vic says something that Evelyn can't catch.

"I don't care," Sherry says. "I just flat don't care."

She disappears into her own next-door room and then Vic wheels himself out, blinking, into the sunlight. He takes a moment to adjust to the light; his wheelchair seems to be tilting or listing. His wheelchair is drunk, thinks Evelyn.

Then Vic sees her, and grins like a cat that has just found a dead bird. "Still here," he says.

"Still here."

"I thought you might have got on your bike and fled."

•

"I could have."

"You might have," Vic says. "Maybe you're just bored. I get bored sometimes."

"Yeah?"

"Hard to believe," he says, "with the *Weekly World News* and the two channels of TV we get. Life in its infinite variety."

His crooked grin, again. The suggestion of a message, again.

But before Evelyn can decode him, Sherry Lewis comes storming out of her little cell with a duffel bag in hand.

"I got my shit," she says. "Let's go."

~   ~   ~

"Don't ask me," Evelyn says. "I mean, they didn't ask me. They just went right ahead and built it."

"Still and all," Vic says.

Evelyn sees it again for the first time through his eyes, remembering her own first time: the log palazzo backed up to the creek, the gables and arches, yards of porches, the log lounges and driftwood drolleries and *what the hell were they thinking*? From a stucco bungalow in Berkeley to this.

"Maybe we'd better not," says Sherry Lewis.

"What?" Evelyn asks her.

"This is a fancy place," Sherry says. "You sure it's OK?"

"I own it," Evelyn says. "Really. I mean, I know it's some kind of fantastic mistake but I do own it. Come in, please."

Sherry looks doubtful but Vic is grinning.

"You've got insurance, right?" he says. "I mean, I'd hate to burn the place down if you didn't."

"Oh, no," Evelyn says. "You do what you want."

"I will, don't worry," Vic says, wheeling himself around to the lift. Sherry is on the deck, looking down at the rushing water, and Evelyn is putting her mother's bike away. OK, she thinks, sending the thought toward her mother, OK but it's a *little* mistake, and one I get to make.

"Girls, I need a hand," Vic says, stalled at the base of the three steps up to the deck. Three little steps and they might as well be a board fence. He doesn't like it, doesn't like to ask, but—Evelyn sees this—Vic has had to learn to submit: a thousand small inconveniences and worse.

"The old heave-ho," Vic says. "One-two-three. Now: no drinking tonight, no dropping of the person on the way out."

"Right," Sherry says. "Speaking of which."

"Come on in," Evelyn says, holding wide the wooden French doors.

"That elk is staring at me," Vic says, inside.

"He stares at everyone," Evelyn says. "It's the glass eyes, they follow you around the room."

"I'm going to have a little drink," Sherry says; sits down on the big leather sofa, cracks the bottle of Jack Daniel's, washes down a decent swallow with beer.

Vic wheels himself around to the dining table, under the antler chandelier. He looks strangely mute and humble, a sorrow making its way through him.

"Who wants dinner?" Evelyn says.

"Not me," Sherry Lewis says, taking another pull at the Jack Daniel's. "I'm a little tired, actually."

"You want to eat something," Vic tells her.

"Don't tell me what I want."

"I can't carry you out of here," he says.

"I didn't ask you to."

Vic stares—and Evelyn notices that she has disappeared from the room again, that Sherri and Vic are alone, inside that sealed sphere. A *couple*. Everything is code for something else.

"I'll start the grill," says Evelyn, leaving the two of them in her parents' house, with the good china and Remington bronzes (from Costco but still). Out onto the deck, out into the rush of cold water over rocks, the enveloping sound and the cool spray of mist, she drags the cover off the big Weber and lights it. The dutiful daughter. She feels ripped off. If Vic wasn't interested, if he wasn't there for *her*, what was he there for at all? She edges closer to the open window, out of sight, listening.

"Who's going to drive you home?" Vic is asking her. "Who's going to get you out of here?"

"You can take care of her," Sherri says. At least, this is what Evelyn thinks she says. Over the wind, the rushing stream, it all sounds alike, too faint to finally make out.

"This isn't the right day," Vic says, or something like it.

"Oh, *fuck* you," Sherri says.

This time Evelyn is sure—not the words but the tone, the intimacy, the bitterness only couples can get, when they think nobody's listening. Evelyn is alone again.

It's exactly evening: the sun gone down, the sky deepening

toward blue. Evelyn walks off into the cut grass in front of the house, listening to the creek, which goes and goes and never gets anywhere. It's beautiful, the color of the sky and the lonely line of trees, and Evelyn feels special for seeing it. They are inside, the two of them, and she is out here alone. But she is seeing this, this beautiful evening, and they are not. Evelyn is special.

~   ~   ~

Sherry Lewis has passed out on the sofa, when Evelyn comes back in. The bottle is empty on the coffee table. Vic is rummaging through her father's 33s.

"Is she OK?" Evelyn asks.

"This is great," Vic says. "These are so great!"

"What?"

"Look at this—Fred McDowell, Son House, Furry Lewis. Don't you wish that was your name? Hey Furry, what's happening?"

"Is she OK?"

"Her?" Vic says, like there was anybody else Evelyn could be talking about. "Sherry's had a hard day."

"She's not going to die or anything, is she? That's a lot of whiskey, isn't it?"

"Sherry's OK for tonight."

"If you say so," Evelyn says, watching the tan flesh of Sherry's stomach (her tank top has ridden up) rise and fall with each slow breath.

A desperate moaning arises out of the speaker cabinets and then, somewhere far in the background, a strange, thin, whining guitar.

"What the hell is that?" Evelyn asks.

Vic glares at her, like somebody talking in church, then lowers his head into the music again.

" 'Dark Was the Night, Cold Was the Ground,' " Vic says, when the music is done.

"What?"

"That's the name of the song," Vic says. "Blind Willie Johnson. That's the Old Testament right there, baby. You don't know him?"

"I don't know anything," Evelyn says. "I mean, that's my dad's record."

"How old are you, anyway?"

Evelyn feels herself blush. "None of your business," she says.

"I don't mean," he says. "I just lose track. You know, you wake up one day and Reagan is in the White House and the next thing you know it's this asshole Clinton."

"Maybe you should pay attention."

"I'm sorry every time I do."

A fresh round of groaning and guitar playing erupts from the speakers. Without being asked, Vic leans toward the volume knob and turns it down. The sky is black outside.

"Let me fix you dinner," Evelyn says.

"Those trout might be spoilt, sitting in the ice like that," he says.

"They don't smell bad."

"They're probably all right then, long as they don't smell. You don't want me to smoke in here, do you?"

Fine with me but my mom won't go for it, Evelyn thinks; then, *my mother is dead.* What does Evelyn herself want?

She says, "Go ahead, but open a window or something. I've got real-estate people coming through anytime. They don't give you any notice at all, they just come barging in."

"Well, it's your house, isn't it? Tell them to cut it out."

"Not if I want to sell the place. Which I do. I never even lived here."

"Where are you from, anyway?"

"Nowhere," Evelyn says. "California. Plus we moved around a lot. Where are you from?"

"I'm from right here," Vic says. "Twenty years trying to get the fuck out of this valley and now every millionaire from Texas to California wants my Rocky Mountain high. Not that I'm pissed or anything."

"Go ahead and smoke," Evelyn tells him, a little scared, feeling his evil radiation. "Anywhere, anytime you want."

She flees into the kitchen, then—a moment later—hears the patio door open, then close again behind him: alone. But standing at the sink, slitting open the silvery bellies of the trout and draining their guts into the disposal, she feels the way the valence of the house has changed, just with living people in it, people besides herself. She can imagine Sherry breathing in the next room. She's making dinner, and after a while Vic will come in and sit with her, and there will be quiet and calm. She knows she's pretending. But still it feels good, just to know they are there, to know that she is not alone for once.

She hears the patio door slide shut, the rubbery squish of wheelchair wheels on polished wood floors behind her, but she doesn't turn. She doesn't want to spoil the moment.

He doesn't stop, though—rolls his chair right up alongside her and stops and rests his head against the curve of her hip, the roll of flesh where her back meets her ass. She can feel him breathing down there. She feels that first moment of panic— she's fat! she's making a fool of herself!—but then, for a moment, it's just nice, nice and quiet.

"What's that?" she asks him.

"Nothing to worry about," Vic says, straightening up, rolling away. "It was just something I wanted to do. I get blue this hour of the day."

"Sure," she says. She understands: the last light in the sky, the day slipping by like water through her fingers.

"Let me make this for you," Evelyn says, and Vic moves all the way away, takes up a station at the kitchen table and drinks a beer held between two fists, watching the sky outside. Evelyn is making a salad, some couscous out of a box, a souvenir of a trip to the food co-op in Kalispell, where she saw people who were a little like her, though they were all older, and many of them were hippies.

~   ~   ~

"What Sherry said," Vic says, digging in with his fork, trout, couscous, "did she tell you? Her and Lynn were identical twins. And I was married to Lynn, though not at the time."

You got married after she died? Evelyn thinks. She says, "Help me with the math on that."

"It's easy," Vic says. "We got married and then we got divorced and then we were fixing to get married again, though it was taking us a while to get around to it. It seemed like an experience we had both had."

"Though not for the second time," Evelyn says, and Vic grins.

It thrills her, sitting there, talking about marriage like she knows what she's talking about. He's *paying attention* to her.

"A series of mistakes," Vic says, "though they didn't seem fatal at the time."

"It hasn't slowed you down much."

Vic brightens. "Why would it? Look, I know something you don't."

This is after dinner, still in the kitchen, the quiet of the big house all around them.

"What?" she asks him.

"Right at the end, there? with the van rolling over and over and on into the ditch, you know, I was drunk before it happened but then I sobered up perfectly fine and even better than fine, everything slowed down and I could feel everything and understand everything and I even had time to think about it—my Moment of Clarity, one per lifetime is all you get, I understand, but in my Moment of Clarity I saw that it would be really easy to just let go, you know?"

"I don't know," Evelyn says. For some reason, this is making her angry.

"It's not like there aren't enough people," Vic says. "It's not like I've done all that great with the chances I've had. I mean, you work and work and you struggle, because you're supposed to. I mean, *I love life,* you know? What a fucking bore. It's like rooting for General Motors or Budweiser."

Vic looks happier than he's looked all day, grinning at her, gripping the can of beer between his fisted hands and drinking.

"You must be pretty impressed with yourself," says Evelyn. It's like he's showing off. It's like he's making fun of her. It's not exactly anything. She goes around to her parents' liquor cabinet and pours herself a tiny glass of goo, some orange-flavored liqueur that is the sweetest thing she's ever put in her mouth.

"Well, what?" he says, and Vic is pissed off, too. "I'm supposed to do what? put the idea away, like it's poison or something. Put the toothpaste back in the tube."

"No," she says, starting to hear him. Softening.

"All these automatic feelings," he says. "I mean, don't get on your high horse. You never have a bad thought?"

"All the time."

"You ever ask yourself, what if the bad thoughts are true? What if those nice, happy thoughts are just ways of fooling yourself? Look," he says, "nobody's watching, nobody's keeping score. Nobody gives a shit. If you're not enjoying yourself, right? I mean, these kids you see in the paper with leukemia or something, the valiant struggle for life, you know, what a bag of shit. Let 'em go! Five years of pain with no hair, so the rest of us can stand around like fucking cheerleaders, life is good! Life is good!'"

"That was a long moment," Evelyn says. There's a taste like pennies in her mouth, a sense that she shouldn't be listening.

"Well," he says, "I had a while in the hospital to think it over. There wasn't much all else to do."

"No," she says.

"Not even the usual solitary pursuits," he says, and grins. "I couldn't get the nurses to help."

"I'm drunk," Evelyn announces, and it's true: the evening is collapsing around her like a wet cake, her brain has gone all damp and spongy and flat. The last glass of liqueur still coats her throat, like pancake syrup. She says, "I'm drunk and I'm tired."

"Not me," Vic says. "Been half drunk since about eleven-thirty this morning. Half drunk is all I ever get anymore."

"I don't believe you."

"Well, you're right, it's a fucking lie. I do get drunk once in a while."

"I bet."

"Not tonight, though."

Vic wheels himself over to the big French doors and looks out at the creek, which Evelyn knows is sparkling in the yard light. Should she follow or should she not? But this is all over and decided and has been for some time, all but the dithering.

She turns the lights off in the kitchen, all but the soft one over the sink.

She walks over to the stereo and thinks about putting a CD on but she doesn't know this mood, and nothing seems to fit. Vic sits by the window, waiting for her—she can feel it—while she fingers the jewel boxes and ponders: Betty Serveert? Fugazi?

Or there's the quiet. She decides on simple quiet.

She goes over to the French doors and she stands behind Vic and she slips her hand into the open neck of his shirt and leaves her hand there, on the bare skin of his chest. She can feel his breath, rising and falling. A wheelchair handle pokes her in the sternum. This is going to be complicated, no doubt.

Then Vic takes her arm between his two curled hands and gently pulls her hand away from him.

"Ain't going to work," he says.

"What?"

"I haven't got the plumbing for it," Vic says. "Not anymore."

Evelyn feels dizzy, her head all rushing one way and now she's got to stop.

"I don't care," she says. "We could improvise, I guess. Couldn't we?"

A brief moment of pain crosses Vic's face, like Evelyn has accidentally stepped on something. "I guess I'd rather not start," he says. "It's not you."

"No? Who is it, then?"

"You're coming in late, here," Vic says, wheeling around to face her—and it's softness and sadness in his face, true, but also there's something flat and the way he says it. This isn't the first time.

"Thing is," he says, "there's already so much happened. It's just hard, you know?"

"I don't know," Evelyn says, hearing the hard edge in her own voice. But she feels herself disappearing, and she doesn't like it.

"Well," Vic says, "OK, it's not hard, is what I'm saying. The dingus. It don't work."

"Never?"

Vic laughs, not happily.

"Sometimes I wake up in the middle of the night and I'm six inches off the bed," he says. "It's like a piece of railroad steel . . . But there's no predicting."

"Fuck," says Evelyn.

"I don't mean to tease you."

"Then what are you doing here? What are you after, Vic?"

"You invited me," he says quietly. "Where the day takes me, is where I end up. I don't exactly have a plan."

"Just my lucky day," says Evelyn. "In other words."

"Your lucky day," he says, grinning. "It's ending, anyway. You mind if I stay?"

What to do with her hands? What to do with her face? The little fool, the nineteen-year-old baby.

"You can sleep in there," says Evelyn, nodding toward

the dark door of her parents' bedroom, just off the living room; the big double bed where she had planned, vaguely, to take him. Then nods toward Sherry: "She'll be OK?"

"If you've got a blanket, maybe."

"You need a hand?"

Vic blinks at her, like she has tried to take him down, put him in a box. Which was not what she meant, but there's no way to tell him.

"I'll be OK," he says. "Just fine. And thanks for your hospitality."

"Is that a fuck-you?"

"Not even close," he says. "Good night."

And with a squeak and squeal of wheels on polished floor he is gone, alone, and Evelyn is alone in this strangers' house again. Shit, she thinks. Shit shit shit. Something has just happened and she doesn't even know what and this is because she is *nineteen years old* and she doesn't know a fucking thing and shit. And Sherry Lewis asleep there on the couch and the big house closing in around her, as it had all winter. She collects the dinner dishes, dirty plates and forks with grains of couscous stuck in the tines, and she runs the sink full of hot soapy water instead of the dishwasher because she wants something, anything, to do with her hands. If it wasn't for the noise, she'd go out and chop some firewood—the best thing about this past winter, taking the splitting maul and breaking the big rounds of firewood into stove-size chunks, the whack and shatter of the iron head coming down . . . that and the strength she got from it. By winter's end she had real biceps and some other unidentifiable muscles. The feeling that she had out on the deck comes back to her: alone but strong. And stupid, she reminds herself—don't forget stupid.

"What's going on?" asks Sherry Lewis, sleepy.

She's in the kitchen in her tank top and bare feet, her eyes half closed and sleep on her breath. She shakes her head to dust the cobwebs out, then opens Evelyn's refrigerator—without asking—and takes the last Diet Coke.

"Time is it, anyway?" Sherry asks, settling herself at the kitchen table.

"Eleven, eleven-thirty, something like that," Evelyn says.

"Vic out?"

"A few minutes ago."

Sherry yawns, shakes her head again. "It's better that way," she says. "Man! He stays up late sometimes? Gets himself in all kinds of trouble, drinks so much he can't even get out of bed the next day. One time—check this out—he wakes up in the backseat of his friend's car? And the friend's asleep up front? But when Vic wakes him up, they can't get out of the car, not on the driver's side, you know. So Charles, his buddy, gets out the passenger side and sees that the driver's side is all dented up, you know, and he don't remember a thing, and down in that crease he can see there's some paint stuck, and that paint is *school-bus yellow*!"

Evelyn clucks sympathetically.

"So it's a good thing he isn't out and about," Sherry says. "What kind of stories has he been telling you?"

"We were just talking," Evelyn says. She has no intention of telling Sherry anything. I made a fool of myself, she thinks. I am a little ass.

"Two things Vic likes to do," Sherry says. "He loves to drink and he loves to talk. The problem is, he does both, and then he'll say anything."

"No," Evelyn says, "it was nice."

"Well, that's good," Sherry says. "It isn't always." She takes a wet, warm rag from behind the sink, without asking, and starts to clean the counters and the table with it—some unspoken, automatic response, and despite herself, Evelyn is comforted.

"What did he tell you about me?" Sherry asks, too casually.

"Not much," says Evelyn. "He didn't tell me much, now that I think about it. He just talks, doesn't he? just talks to hear the sound of his own voice."

"That's the boy."

"He said you and his wife were twins," Evelyn says. "That made me wonder, you know—what that was like."

"First off, she wasn't his wife, not then," Sherry says, putting the washcloth down to lecture. "Second, we were two-egg twins, we didn't look like each other more than sisters do. Somebody used to ask my father about it, he'd say Lynn was identical but I wasn't at all."

Evelyn looks at her, confused.

"That was a joke," Sherry says.

"No, I know," Evelyn says. Her mind is racing past whatever Sherry says, back to Vic, trying to find something to hold on to, someplace to start. Where was he telling the truth, if ever? What was he trying to say to her?

"He doesn't mean anything by it," Sherry says. "Is there anything left to drink around here?"

"The cooler's on the porch. You could check."

"Maybe I should just quit. I don't know."

"You've been drunk once already, tonight," says Evelyn.

"That's right, I have," says Sherry Lewis, brightening at the thought. "We could just sit for a while, couldn't we? I'm not sleepy at all. Do you mind sitting up with me?"

"I'm wide awake myself," Evelyn lied.

"Then let's go sit," Sherry says. "We can get comfortable in the living room. It's lonely out here, isn't it?"

Evelyn follows her into the living room, then—against her own judgment—steps out onto the deck to get a beer from the cooler. The night is breezy and cool, a big blue moon shining down through the trees, the deck wood cool under her bare feet. Sherry is standing by the door, waiting for her, when she comes back in.

"It's lonely here, isn't it?" she says again, following Evelyn to the big L-shaped sectional, where she sits kitty-corner, watching, as Evelyn pops the top on a last can of Pabst. The sleep has changed Sherry, evened out her looks, or maybe it's the soft lamplight. But her eyes look younger, less dead, her skin looks smooth and full and brown, her face looks alive.

"Have you always lived here?" Evelyn asks.

"I went to college," Sherry says. "I always come back."

"Why?"

"You don't like it here?"

"No I don't," says Evelyn. "It's cold." She stops, thinks for a minute before she goes on, but decides to say it anyway. "It's lonely, too, like you say."

This feels like more than she meant to say, and she wishes—for a second—that she could take it back.

"What brings you back?" Evelyn asks. "Don't you ever just feel like picking up and going?"

"All the time," Sherry says. Without asking, she picks up Evelyn's can of beer and takes a small polite sip from it, then another.

"It's always a story, you know?" says Sherry Lewis. "It's always, you know, my mother dying or the accident. Every time I start to get settled in someplace, there's always some little made-for-TV thing where I've got a part I've got to play. They call me up and I get here, again."

"And here you are," says Evelyn.

"Here I am," Sherry says, and grins. "Too fucking lazy to get off my ass and get moving. I'm going to die here, sweetie, and I don't even know why."

Sherry laughs, and it's an echo of Vic's laugh, something bottomless and black, and Evelyn smiles with a small creepy feeling in her spine.

"What was he like?" Evelyn says. "Before the accident, I mean."

"Like what?"

"I mean, when he could get around and all."

"What did he tell you?"

"Nothing. I mean, I was just . . ."

"He fell out of a tree when he was eleven," Sherry says. "He's been like this ever since."

"But the accident."

"He was driving the van," Sherry says. "That same one we were driving around today, fixed up just like it is. He's had it since he was seventeen."

This seems wrong to Evelyn, something shocking and horrible that he hadn't told her. Death Car, Evelyn thinks.

"And he still drives it?" she asks.

"They wanted to get him a new one," Sherry says. "They declared it totaled? but Vic, he wanted that one back, that same van. He made them build it up again, stem to stern."

"That's fucked."

"You don't know," says Sherry Lewis. "You just don't know."

She turns away, looking briefly out the French doors to where the deck is bathed in blue moonlight, where the pine trees sway. Evelyn's mouth is dry. She takes a sip of her beer. When Sherry turns back, she reaches her hand across the corner of the big sofa and takes Evelyn's hand in hers. It seems incredible—this is really happening, this can't be happening—and then she takes Evelyn's hand and lifts it and kisses the back of it. Evelyn closes her eyes and feels Sherry move up close, next to her on the sofa.

When Evelyn opens her eyes again, Sherry's face is inches away, looking into her eyes.

"Scared?" she says.

Evelyn shakes her head, no, then shrugs: a little.

"You don't have to be scared," says Sherry Lewis, letting her face drift toward Evelyn's, drift toward the kiss, and before her face blurs into softness Evelyn sees her eyes dart away, toward the black, part-open door of her parents' bedroom, the room where Vic is.

Girlfriend Hit by Bus

Oh Christ, says Sage. Oh Jesus, oh fuck. You didn't hear?

Hear what?

I don't want to be the one to tell you.

Billy, in his black kitchen, stares at the telephone, which is also black. The cord looped and spaghettied and splattered with kitchen filth.

What is it?

It's Christa, Sage says. She got hit by a bus.

She was just here, Billy says—because it seems that Sage is telling him that Christa is dead, and this is impossible. She was just here. She was standing in this exact kitchen two hours ago, fighting with him and smoking his cigarettes.

Is she OK? Billy asks, the stupidest question.

No, says Sage.

He can hear her breathing on the other end of the line. She doesn't want to say it. Billy will help her out.

Is she dead, then?

Pretty much, Sage says. I mean, yes, definitely.

What do you mean?

Well, they thought. . . . They had her in the ambulance and all. But I guess it was still too late.

Dead, Billy thinks: another word. He says it to himself, Christa's dead, Christa's dead, trying to convince himself but it's no good. It's just a word.

Do you want me to come over? Sage asks him.

This is where it starts to feel wrong.

No, he says quickly, too quickly. No, I'll call you or come over there. But right now . . .

Are you OK?

Well, no, he thinks. My girlfriend is dead. My ex-girlfriend. Which? They only broke up two hours ago—not time for her to tell anybody. Sage doesn't know, he can tell. Is this for him? Is this Christa being awful, as she could be awful? Run down by a bus. You wouldn't pick it.

Billy?

I'm here, he says.

Do you want me to come over?

Is that what you do? he says. You have coffee? You have drinks? I mean, you're going to have to fill me in on the drill here. This has never happened to me.

Don't be like that.

Like what?

Like you are, Sage says.

Can I see her?

Fuck, I don't know, Sage says. You could ask the hospital, I guess.

Which one?

The one on Twenty-first, she says, right down the street. What's its name?

I'm going over there, Billy says. I'll talk to you.

He hangs up on her and waits to feel it, the big feeling he knows is coming. He's known Christa since they were both six. But he's not running to her, he's not crying. Billy has to piss but Jon, the roommate, is in the downstairs bathroom shaving his head and Cherry, another, is taking one of her three-hour baths upstairs.

Who was that? Jon asks.

Nobody, Billy says. Nothing.

Like telling it would make it real. He holds the feeling close inside his chest but he can't feel it, stands in the backyard in the Oregon drizzle, pissing on a rosebush, thinking: Christa's dead. Dead. No she isn't.

There's something wrong with him. He can't feel a thing. He knows he should be feeling something but he isn't.

Out into the streets in his leather jacket. He wishes he could think of some other way to look. He used to scare people, but now they look right through him, the four o'clock rush on Twenty-third Street, people buying books, people buying flowers. Christa, though—he lets himself think about her, what he loved about her, trying to generate some kind of feeling—Christa would be flying down the sidewalk, taking up way more room than her skinny body—*body*— would indicate, smoking cigarettes, flame-red hair in a buzz cut and a boy's shirt half-unbuttoned. You could see her little tits if you wanted to. Businessmen and college boys, they all tried.

Christa yelling at him across the street as he walked away from an argument, cars stopping to listen, people coming out onto their porches.

Nothing doing. No feeling. It was like being too drunk and trying to fuck, waiting for something to happen. Maybe I didn't love her, Billy thinks. Maybe I really don't care. Maybe that time was over a while ago, lying awake nights wondering where she was. He was never the only one. This is going to be quite a funeral, he thinks, the casuals and the one-offs and that fucking guitar player who dragged her off to San Francisco that winter, the photographer who gave Christa two hundred dollars to pose and then put her naked on the Internet. Or maybe just him and Sage. He could imagine that, too—the fat friend and the boyfriend in the empty, echoing church with Christa's mother, the priest, Jesus looking down.

Hit by a bus.

This seems completely possible. She never looked when she crossed the street, never owned an umbrella.

The hospital is big and brick, bustling. Inside the smell of cafeteria food and alcohol and the sour damp smell of people in from the rain. Everybody's extra-clean. The woman in white— even Hell needs angels—can't find Christa's name and then she finds it but can't find any current records, only the old ones, an overdose, a bad cut on her arm, a beer bottle some girl threw at her. She clicks through screen after screen, tapping on the monitor with her fingernail.

She came in this afternoon, Billy says. She came by ambulance.

The receptionist's eyes widen a little.

Oh, she says. Was she, uh . . .

What?

Dead? At that time?

I don't know exactly.

She must have been, the receptionist says firmly. That would explain why I can't find her records. We wouldn't have admitted her if that was the case.

Fuck, Billy says—not at the receptionist, no, but just because this was so stupid. A fucking waste.

I'm sorry? she says.

I'm sorry, no, Billy says. I didn't mean . . .

She would be at the city facility in Southeast, says the woman in white. There's most likely an investigation, two or three days is the usual.

The receptionist, or whatever she is, has taken sides against him. The curser. He might be on dope. Behind him, a line of important people whose time he's wasting.

Could you tell me, Billy says. Could I see her?

Are you Mr. Rodriguez?

Who?

The husband.

I don't think there is a husband.

It says here . . .

She taps the screen, and Billy remembers, some dodge, a friend of a friend who couldn't get a green card.

No, he says.

Siblings and spouses, the receptionist says. They don't even like to let them inside. It's a pretty, um, well, it's just a city facility.

Southeast, where?

Eleventh and Belmont, the receptionist says. By the bakery there. OK?

His time is up. His turn is over. He turns from the counter and they are all looking at him, the sick, the relatives of the sick. Christa's in the bakery, and Billy's all by himself and people are staring. I'm special, he thinks. Then remembers that she was already gone, they had their last fight. Things were said that could not be unsaid. People she slept with, opinions of Billy. Somebody's dick in her mouth.

Outside, the spring rain. First greenery on the trees, a little green fuzz or outline on the wet black branches and shoppers hurrying, four-thirty. He stands under the awning at the front of the hospital, the other side from the smokers huddled there. I could go this way, he thinks. I could go that way.

Then Sage drives up in her orange-and-rust Volvo.

She isn't here, he says, climbing in and then wishing he hadn't. Sage is crying. Her black eyeliner is running down her face in black streaks. This makes him angry, for some reason, all this girly feeling, tears and makeup.

She isn't here, he says again. What do you want to do?

Where is she?

Some kind of place in Southeast, he says. A bakery.

What?

By the bakery, there on Belmont.

She pulls the rotting Volvo out into the traffic and they sit. Somebody's trying to park, somebody without driving talent. The intermittent wipers work only part of the time, starting and stopping across the windshield at random.

They won't let us in, Billy says. They won't let us see her.

Why not?

It's just family. That's what they told me at the hospital.

I want to see her, Sage says.

I know you do but you can't.

I want to see her, Sage says, louder, like he didn't hear the first time. And there's something in her voice, some note like paper tearing, it goes right through him. It's the feeling. Sage's got it and he doesn't and there's something wrong with him.

We'll never make it, Billy says.

Where?

We'll never make it to Southeast before five, he says. Not in the rain.

What's so special about five? she asks. I mean, a place like that, they don't close. People stop dying at five o'clock, I mean, I don't think so.

I want a drink, Billy says.

That's not going to help.

Oh, yes it is, he says—and he can feel it, longs for it right now, the big swimming spinning drunk. Christa will make a perfect excuse for a big drunk, days of drunk. The car is fifty feet from where they started and not moving again.

Park, he says.

I want to see her, Sage says again. I want to see Christa.

She got hit by a bus, Billy says.

Maybe this coldness inside him is all that he is, all that he's got. There's a kind of pleasure in saying.

She got hit by a bus, he says. She won't be pretty, even if they let us see her, which they won't, and besides . . .

Besides what?

I don't know. It's fucked up.

What?

We broke up, he says. This morning.

It turns out he can say anything, anything at all, and not feel anything but the coldness inside. Faces on the sidewalk, white blurs passing by in the rain. Everybody has money now.

Sage says, I give up.

She turns the car around in the street—a six-point turn with the oncoming cars blowing their horns at her—then up a side street until she sees a parking spot and in and turns to Billy.

Cocksucker, she says.

You think I killed her? Billy says. I didn't.

But he's lying, or doesn't know if he's lying—they both hear it.

It was different this time, he says. I don't know.

You are supposed to take care of the people you love, she says.

What if they don't want to be taken care of?

It doesn't matter, Sage says. You have to anyway.

What if they fucking hate being taken care of? What if it's the one thing you know will run them right out the door?

You know it doesn't matter, Sage says.

She reaches for the door and leaves him sitting there in the rain, Sage the beautiful fat girl all in black. He's just going to sit there. He's going to wait for it, whatever it is.

Christa's dead.

It's still just words.

Kids drew pictures on the sidewalk next to the car, faces in chalk that are melting in the rain, flowers turning gray in the afternoon light and rain. Ho-ho, he thinks. The whole world is sad like me.

But then he wants to see her dresses, smell her sweat and perfume and smoke. He wants to be in Christa's room. Her mother will come and take it all away, sell what she can and throw out the rest, her mother always always needs the money. Christa's mother, still alive. The boyfriend, the fat friend, the mother. He wants to lie on her dirty sheets, see if he can find something of hers to steal before the mother takes all of it.

Five-fifteen. He's supposed to be at work. Even the word, the idea of "work" seems to come from some other place that's strange to him and he understands, for the first time, that something has happened today, something has already happened.

Demicoli will fire his ass again.

Lewis and Clark, he thinks in the liquor store. Cheap gin to scour him out and purify him, the green light of a cheap-gin hangover, anything. Draw the curtain. Turn the page.

Sage is already there in Christa's room when he gets there. She's got one of the other rooms in the house, the two women and two boys in a band, the band on tour; the house lightless, heatless, empty. Sage is sitting on the mattress on the floor where Christa slept when she slept at home. In the delicate half-light her face is almost beautiful. No, it is—it is beautiful. There's something terrible in her face, some real feeling that has hollowed out the angles of her cheeks and lit her eyes. Her features—all oversize—suddenly fit together and she looks terrifying and powerful like a Greek goddess. A handful of lightning bolts.

Billy is scared of her, a little. He cracks the bottle and drinks, a ribbon of warm fire down his throat, then offers her the bottle and she takes it, and drinks.

I wish, she says, and then she stops.

What?

I wish I had a television, she says, and lights a cigarette. I wish I had three televisions, like Elvis.

I've got a TV, Billy says. You can come over and watch it.

In a minute, maybe, she says. Thanks.

Christa in the afternoons, on this mattress, this one right here. She would sleep till eleven or twelve or sometimes never, the night stretching out till morning and into the afternoon, the time Hayley got a bottle of blue pills, nobody knew what they were but they would keep you going for as long as you kept taking them. Then the two-day crash when they ran out. Christa when her brother died crosslegged, naked, leaning against the wall. She didn't talk for two days. That was sorrow. Where was his? It's coming, he can feel it. Not yet but soon.

Did she come?

What?

Sage is standing in the closet now, touching fabrics, a red dress Billy had never seen her wear, a series of white shirts.

When you had sex, she says, did she come?

Usually, Billy says, though what he really means is *sometimes*, her skinny little resistant body, the way it had to be coaxed and flattered and then sometimes, and then sometimes not, and other times he would end up sore and alone on his end of the bed.

The one time we tried, says Sage. It was like I had the magic touch, you know? Like I knew exactly what to do. I never feel like that, not with anybody else.

I didn't know.

Sage looks up, surprised.

You didn't know what?

I didn't know you were one of them, he says. I knew there were girls.

Not so many. Not like you'd think, to look at her. I mean, she liked it. Am I bothering you?

No, he says. Why?

But he was shaken out of his little dream, his little meditation on how much of her he never owned, how much he never even knew about. She liked it.

It's just what I'm thinking about, Sage says. It's what I feel like. You know what I feel like?

No.

I feel like this, she says, and takes her big arm with the thorn tattoo and sweeps the top of Christa's dresser onto the floor, the concert-ticket stubs and perfume bottles, photographs and lipsticks, the travel alarm, the Barbie heads all landing and rattling on the wood floor, scattering glass.

Then everything stops movement all at once and it's quiet again and nothing has happened. Then Sage is slumped on the bed, a big puddle of her weeping. If he can't feel it now, he's never going to feel it. He goes to sit beside her on the bed. He puts his arm around her back and feels the rack and heave of her huge sobs and then the smaller hiccupy sobs as she quiets. Gray light and quiet, the moment when afternoon tips into evening and then it's nearly dark. Rain on the roof, tapping on the glass. Rain on the bushes outside.

Just a numbness. Two thicknesses of skin and clothes away,

Sage *is* all the way inside it and still he can't feel a thing. The way she looks: terrible, beautiful.

Just the nothing.

Sage gets to be terrible and beautiful and Billy gets to be nothing. He reaches past her, takes the bottle and drinks, hands it to Sage and she drinks like it was the last water on Earth. The light running out. Nothing means anything, nothing matters.

He reaches and touches Sage's breast through her shirt. She looks up at his face but she doesn't stop him. The armament of her brassiere.

Don't, she says.

I want to.

Don't, she says. Please.

But her voice is already drunk and dazed, and when he looks into her little dark eyes he sees that they have already glazed over, lost in touch.

Oh, she says.

All the permission Billy needs. Under Sage's skirt, her legs are long and full and smooth-skinned, heavy in his hand, and then she's touching back, and then it's like high school—a tangle of jeans and shirts and underwear and somewhere the skin. A big girl, Sage is. Folds and ripples. She's weeping under him, a small catlike sound, and Billy is touching her, inside her, knowing how different from Christa she is—the small body, flat breasts, ungenerous and stubborn—and he can hardly wait to tell her. O guess what Sage did? he will say. Guess what happened the day you died? And this is exactly the kind of evil story Christa loves, she loves misbehavior, violations of decency, here they are, they are giving death the finger and Christa will love that except that she will never know. Christa's dead. He suddenly understands that she will never be alive again. He will never get a chance to tell her; Christa, who would have loved this story so much.

ALSO BY KEVIN CANTY

INTO THE GREAT WIDE OPEN

*"A stunning, sensual novel that brings adolescence to its highest
state of grace."* —Los Angeles Times Book Review

Into the Great Wide Open is the story of two young people flee-
ing their families' emotional abandonment to find refuge in each
other. With his mother in an institution and his father a distant
alcoholic, Kenny Kolodny hangs on the periphery of his world,
until he makes a passionate connection with the troubled, beautiful, fiercely-independent Junie Williamson. Through their
highly-charged, erotic relationship, Kenny simultaneously enters
"the life of the body" and rises beyond it into self-sacrificing ten-
derness. In spare but lyrical prose, Canty revives the heady
carnival of adolescence, evoking its confusing emotional landscape and its heightened sensuality.

Fiction/Literature/0-679-77652-4

NINE BELOW ZERO

*"Smart, gritty, unsentimental. . . . Finely tuned to the precari-
ousness and treachery of human need."* —The New York Times

Set against the unrelenting landscape of the American West, *Nine
Below Zero* is a penetrating exploration of reckless love. Marvin
Deernose, a Native American carpenter and recovering alcoholic,
has just returned to his Montana hometown with hopes of finding a new start. Early one snowy morning, Marvin notices an
overturned Cadillac down an embankment. After rescuing the
elderly Senator Henry Neihart, who has just suffered a stroke,
Marvin is invited to the Senator's estate where he is immediately
drawn to Justine Gallego, the Senator's wayward, unhappily
married granddaughter. As these tarnished souls recognize their
profound, shared attraction, they dive headlong into a dangerous
and intense affair that forever alters the course of their lives.

Fiction/Literature/0-375-70799-9

"A darkly nuanced, exquisite first collection of stories. Canty navigates the many gulfs and eddies of skewed relationships with unflinching concentration." —Entertainment Weekly

The men and women in this collection of short stories walk a thin line. On one side are well-lit homes, steady jobs, love, or its approximation. On the other side lies chaos. To step across takes only one false move, one bad choice. The summons to do the wrong thing may come from a neighbor with the body of a grown woman and the mind of a submissive child. It may come from the ex-wife who shows up just when you've gotten over her. Disaster may take the form of a drunk driver who carries a gun in his glove compartment—a gun that one of you will have to use before the night is over. *A Stranger in This World* offers us a catalog of risk in stories that unveil the hazards at the heart of American lives.

Fiction/Literature/0-679-76394-5

VINTAGE CONTEMPORARIES
Available at your local bookstore, or call toll-free to order:
1-800-793-2665 (credit cards only).